Mary H. Tennyson

Friend Perditus

Vol. II

Mary H. Tennyson

Friend Perditus
Vol. II

ISBN/EAN: 9783337065980

Printed in Europe, USA, Canada, Australia, Japan

Cover: Foto ©Andreas Hilbeck / pixelio.de

More available books at **www.hansebooks.com**

FRIEND PERDITUS

𝔄 𝔑𝔬𝔳𝔢𝔩

BY

MARY H. TENNYSON

𝔍𝔫 𝔗𝔴𝔬 𝔙𝔬𝔩𝔲𝔪𝔢𝔰

VOL. II.

LONDON: CHAPMAN AND HALL
LIMITED
1891

WESTMINSTER :

PRINTED BY NICHOLS AND SONS,

25, PARLIAMENT STREET.

FRIEND PERDITUS.

CHAPTER I.

THE next three months were so crowded with business that I really had no time for gloomy reflections. In the first place I commenced negociations with the firm of Simpson, Marshall and Co., and ultimately, persuading them to accept a hundred and eighty thousand in place of the two hundred thousand they had originally asked, I became a partner in that most prosperous business, with a yearly income, according to the estimated profits of the house, of thirty-five thousand pounds.

Mr. Stanniwell had sold my shares even

to greater advantage than he anticipated, and, after paying this hundred and eighty thousand, I found that I had still eighty thousand pounds remaining.

Twenty thousand of this I deposited at the bank to draw upon, and the rest I invested in Government securities, determined that no matter what might happen to me in business, my mother and brother should be absolutely secured from want in the future.

My mother was not well pleased that I would not at once settle upon her and Lucien twenty thousand pounds each out of this fund, and in all probability I should have given in to her wishes on the subject had not Frank Nesbit and Charlie Hall combated the notion so strongly.

They represented to me that I should be acting most unwisely to do anything of the sort; for, in the event of my marrying at any future time, and having perhaps children to provide for, as well as a wife, it would be doing them the greatest injustice, in case of any business disaster overtaking me, to have made this disposition of so large an amount of money.

Seeing that I still hesitated, in his true friendship for me, Charles Hall, who was by no means a favourite of my mother's, actually suggested that he should go and speak to her on the subject, and open her eyes to the unreasonable nature of her request.

This earnestness on his part decided me. I could not afford to neglect his counsel, he had always been so wise an adviser to me; and, even if he had been less clever, his absolute integrity and good faith would have invested his opinion with a golden weight.

Therefore I told my mother that I could not do what she asked, but while my business prospered I was willing to allow her one thousand pounds a year for private expenses, and my brother also could draw upon me to a similar extent. In the event of Lucien's marrying, I undertook to increase his portion by another thousand a year, always supposing that things went well with me in business. In any other case, of course, another arrangement must be come to.

My mother fretted and fumed for some time over this, but at length, when she saw that I was firmly resolved, she ceased to importune me.

Having signed an agreement with the firm, I next turned my attention to finding a suitable house.

My mother's ideas on this subject were most magnificent, but fortunately my brain is very clear where money is concerned, and I perceived at once that even with so considerable an income as forty thousand a year, it would be the height of folly to take a house that happened to be empty in Park Lane, or a magnificent mansion in Palace Gardens, either of which I might have had at a yearly rental of three thousand pounds.

At last I discovered a residence which appeared to me to be everything we could desire

in size and situation. It stood in Brook
Street, Mayfair, and I considered it well worth
the nine hundred pounds a year the landlord wanted for it. From basement to
attic the appointments were faultless, and
the place having been entirely re-decorated
by a well-known artist in this line, even
in its empty condition it looked cheerful
and inviting.

Although this house was not quite so
palatial as my mother desired it to be,
and, in her opinion, the marble staircase
leading from the hall might have been a
trifle wider with advantage, still—" It would
do very well," she said calmly, and thereupon I settled matters with the landlord,
inwardly marvelling at the wonderful power
of adapting themselves to circumstances
some women possess. Here was my mother,
for instance. who five short weeks before had
been living in a condition of absolute squalor,
examining with an air of most critical coolness rooms and decorations that struck even
Charles Hall who, by this time had got

into very fashionable practice, as being singularly fine in proportion and elegant in design.

Lucien was a striking example of how much inferior men are to women with respect to this capability of adapting themselves to novel surroundings. He made no pretence of not being surprised and impressed, and I must admit, though possibly my mother's attitude was the more dignified, and calculated to awe the swarms of tradesmen who, even in this aristocratic neighbourhood, pestered us with efforts to secure our future custom, I was much better pleased with his outspoken admiration than I was with her condescending patronage.

Altogether I found my brother Lucien far easier to get on with than my mother. He was much less blunt and brusque than she was, and I saw that out of consideration for me he often tried to check her when she said or did things solely with the intention of wounding what she called my 'false delicacy and squeamish nonsense.'

Lucien had not much influence with her, but I was grateful for the effort he made to spare me, and moreover his conduct on the subject of the settlements had been very conciliatory. He had shown no gleam of annoyance when I declined to do what our mother proposed, and I appreciated his good temper the more when I witnessed the burst of anger with which she received the first intimation of my resolve.

Being desirous of restoring her completely to good humour, I called at the hotel on the evening that I had finally settled with the landlord.

" Now, mother," I said cheerfully, " the house is waiting for us ; it only wants furnishing."

" Give me enough money and I'll take that trouble off your hands," she cried eagerly.

" The very thing I was going to pro-

pose," I replied. " I want to get into harness
in the city. You see I have to learn my
trade, and if you and Lucien would undertake the furnishing I should be glad.
Order what you like, and have the bills
sent in to me to pay."

" I would rather go with the money in
my hand to buy things," replied my mother
shrewdly; "people charge much more when
they give you credit."

This certainly sounded reasonable, so I
took out my pocket-book and drew a cheque
for a thousand pounds.

" Make that go as far as you can," I said,
" but if you require more you must have it.
Remember, mother, I want a house that
looks like a home."

With this weighty matter arranged, I
imagined, I plunged myself heart and soul
into my new business. On the fourth
morning, however, when I left Charlie's
house—Charlie's now entirely, for I had
formally relinquished my share on quarter
day, insisting on his accepting my half of

the furniture as a wedding present—when I left the house and bent my steps towards the station, I encountered Lucien, who, cigar in mouth, was strolling up and down in the bright May sunlight, evidently waiting for me.

" Why didn't you come in ? " I said, when I had shaken hands. " Have you breakfasted ? "

" Oh, yes, an hour ago ; the mater was off shopping early. I didn't come in because I wanted a word with you without Hall's being present."

" Yes—nothing wrong, is there ? "

He hesitated, and again I saw the disagreeable furtive expression in his eyes which had impressed me so unfavourably on our first meeting.

" No, I don't know that there is, still I thought I had better mention the subject to you."

" What is it ?   Come, Lucien, surely it can't be so difficult a matter ? "

" Well, it isn't exactly a pleasant one,

because it looks as if I were running our mother down, and I don't want to appear to do that."

"Of course not," I replied, wondering what in the world he could be going to say.

"Well, the long and the short of it is," he continued with an effort, "I am afraid you have acted a little unwisely in commissioning mother to buy the furniture for the new house."

"But why?"

"Why mother's tastes are—well, to speak plainly—rather loud; to tell truth there is no denying the fact that our mother is rather loud altogether; moreover she is evidently not inclined to let me have a word with regard to the selection of the things, or I might tone down her love of glitter and bright colours a bit. However, I can't explain to you what I mean better than by showing you one or two specimens that are in a window in Tottenham Court Road of the drawing-room furniture that she has

ordered. If you have half an hour to spare
this morning you had better take a cab and
see for yourself, and then, if you don't
approve, it would be as well to put a stop
to her proceedings before she has gone any
further."

I called a hansom, and as we drove along
I could not help wondering what made this
such a difficult subject for my brother to
approach. It was no such rank heresy that
I could see to doubt his mother's taste, and
yet, judging from his white, nervous face,
one might almost suppose that he had been
accusing her of some crime.

Lucien ordered the driver to stop at a
certain shop in Tottenham Court Road, and
no sooner did I look into the window than
I gave a gasp of downright horror. Of all
the atrocious coverings that the mind of
man ever conceived, surely none could possibly equal that particular, terrible, scarlet
satin ; and, as if the predominant colour
were not sufficiently distressing to the eye,
the glaring vulgarity of the furniture was in-

creased tenfold by the fact that in the centre
of each chair-back and seat there flaunted
some gorgeous tropical bird in raised silks.
Parrots, macaws, and every imaginable fowl
of the air who boasted a vivid, not to say
coarse-coloured plumage, glared at the be-
holder with menacing glass eyes, and seemed,
with hooked beaks, and raised defiant claws
to threaten with an instant and terrible
vengeance anyone who should approach them
too nearly.

"Good heavens!" I cried. "You can't
mean to tell me, Lucien, that our mother
has ordered those awful things for our
drawing-room?"

He nodded.

"And the carpet is royal blue, with great
bunches of scarlet flowers on it," he continued. "Mother thinks the contrast will
be charming with the gold frames of the
chairs and sofas."

"But it's all so terribly common and
gaudy," I continued, in tones of thorough
disgust. "Why, in the name of goodness,
didn't our mother go to a good shop? I

really should not have thought it would be possible to buy anything so violently offensive as this in London."

"I fancied you wouldn't like them," he replied laconically, gazing disapprovingly at the outrageous birds.

"Like them! I don't pretend to be over fastidious, but I couldn't live in a room with such fiendish creatures. Fancy resting one's back against that diabolical parrot there. It's eye is positively devilish."

"Well, you had better come and tell mother so. Don't say that I put you up to it, Friend, or she'll be furious with me. Pretend that you met me by accident here, and that I showed you the things."

"All right," I said. "I don't want to get you into trouble, Lucien, and really I am grateful to you for having opened my eyes. Why," I continued, laughing—though I was chagrined, I could not help seeing a certain humorous side to the situation — "why, our house would have been the talk of the town if the rest of its furniture had been in keeping with the drawing-room suite."

But before I reached the Alexandra Hotel I lost sight of all the comicality of the matter, and, looking into Lucien's face, I said uneasily :

"I am afraid our mother won't be pleased at my taking this furnishing business out of her hands."

"I am *sure* she will not," he replied. "That's where the difficulty comes in. Mother is fond of spending money, and she won't like returning what she has left of the thousand pounds, I know."

I drew down the corners of my lips. It was a stiff sum to lose; but anything was better than having either a quarrel with my mother or my home made horrible to me. With a shrug of the shoulders, I replied :

"Well, if she objects strongly to refunding I must make the best of it. I shouldn't argue the matter for long. Fortunately, a thousand more or less is not of vital importance to me."

At this the cloud that had hung over my brother's face disappeared as if by magic, and all the rest of the way he chatted as though in the brightest and merriest of moods.

As I expected, my mother received my proposal to complete the furnishing of the house myself in a very angry spirit; but, rendered more acute than usual by Lucien's hint, I perceived at once that her grievance was the having to return me the unspent money.

"You are placing me in a horribly undignified position, Friend," she grumbled. "I am sure I don't know what I shall say to the man in Tottenham Court Road. I had actually bought the furniture and ordered the carpet. I dare say it is half made by this time, and the bill was to be a heavy one, I can assure you. If you are so dreadfully averse to cheerful surroundings, you ought to have told me of your peculiarity."

Cheerful surroundings! And she described those fearful feathered creatures, disporting on their lurid scorching backgrounds as cheerful surroundings!

" Any way," my mother continued, with increasing annoyance, " I can't give you nearly the whole of the thousand pounds back, I shall have to persuade the man to buy the furniture and carpet of me again, and of course he won't do so at its original value."

" Well, mother," I said in a propitiatory tone, " I am really very sorry to have placed you in a such a disagreeable situation, and I am also sorry that our tastes don't agree. Under the circumstances, therefore, I should not think of adding to your perplexities. Pay the man what he wants to let you off the bargain, and spend what remains on anything you like."

I was not as a rule very observant of other people. I hope this does not argue that there was any very superabundant amount of egotism in my nature at this period; I do not think it does; I rather imagine it was the outcome of my peculiar mental condition, which was very conducive to a system of profound self-analysis; but unobservant as I was, I could not fail to notice, on the conclusion of my speech, a quick furtive interchange of glances between my mother and Lucien, who up to this moment had stood with his back towards us, as if determined to take no part in the discussion.

On my way to Gillow's, into whose capable hands I decided to put the entire furnishing of my house, I puzzled myself with conjectures as to the meaning of this intercepted very peculiar glance, until at last I became quite worried with it. My conversation with one of the head men at Gillow's interrupted the course of my thoughts for a time, but when I started citywards in a hansom my mind reverted to the subject again.

"What could they mean, I wonder?" I thought, and then an explanation of their mysterious conduct, though not a very satisfactory one, occurred to me.

"I should not be surprised," I muttered, "if after all the furniture were not expensive, that Lucien knew it, and was aware also that my mother pretended she had paid a heavy sum for it to make her grievance appear more weighty. Well, if that is so, it was not an honourable trick, to say the least of it."

But no sooner had I spoken than I began to reproach myself.

" I am getting dreadfully suspicious," I murmured; " I have no right to suppose any such thing ; the expression that passed between them no doubt was only a gleam of satisfaction at the acquisition of more money. Well, there is nothing absolutely wrong in that, and since they know so well the misery of poverty, and the bitter sordid cares connected with want of money, I ought to be the last one in the world to reproach them with an undue appreciation of it. I, too, whose mind so short a time ago, with no such excuse as theirs, was filled to the exclusion of every better thought, with the love of gain."

But though I argued I did not succeed in convincing myself; really and truly in my heart of hearts I believed I had been deceived as to the worth of the furniture, and I chafed and fumed under the imposition.

By the time I reached the end of Tottenham Court Road I had made up my mind.

Desiring the cabman to alter his course, I was once more driven to the shop which contained the objects of my aversion, and a little shiver of disgust passed over me as I noticed that quite a crowd were gathered together on the pavement in front of the shop, gazing at the fiendish birds, and commenting upon them in a very satirical and derisive manner.

Entering the shop I asked for the manager.

" Can you tell me," I said, trying to keep out of my countenance any expression of disapproval, " what would be the price of a suite of furniture similar to that you are displaying in the window?"

An unmistakable smile of amusement flitted across the man's serious business-like face.

" Do you allude to the birds and scarlet satin and gold ? " he inquired, still with a broad grin, which he struggled in vain to subdue.

" Yes," I replied, wondering at his peculiar manner, " I do."

" Well then, sir, no money could buy a similar set to that."

" Indeed ! " I cried, in amazement.

" You see, sir, this is how it is : I am simply displaying that suite of furniture in my shop window for a day or two to attract attention in the neighbourhood; it really never occurred to me that any Englishman would be likely to desire one on the same pattern—they make my eyes ache every time I look at them."

I coloured. I was really mortified that this man should consider me capable of a wish to possess such hideous vulgar things; and noticing my vexation he continued quickly, with the idea of appeasing my just indignation—

" Of course I admit they are very handsome, and the upholstery work and the gilding of the frames are really first rate. You are evidently a good judge of such matters, sir, and I wish I could execute your order; but I cannot if you are set upon that particular design. That suite of furniture has been made by us according to instructions received, and is now the property of a Persian prince, who takes it to his native country next week as a present to his favourite wife. When I received the order, Prince Abdul Nasrin made it a *sine quâ non* that I was not to reproduce the design, which is his own, for our benefit. I assure you, sir, I am sorry to have to disappoint you, as another order such as this would have been a capital one for me —the Prince pays me five hundred pounds for this suite."

I did not feel up to business in the City after this—I could not make it out—so, dismissing the cab, I strolled to the Park, and walked gently in the direction of Wilton Crescent. By the time I reached my home

I fancied I had found the solution of the mystery.

Probably my mother had inquired the price of the furniture, and from what passed between them had imagined the man understood her desire to purchase the things; but in that case why should my presumed admiration for them have occasioned him so much surprise? Then I remembered his remark about not having expected any such application from an Englishman, and I concluded he referred to my mother's inquiry, my mother, who certainly could not have been mistaken for an Englishwoman by any stretch of imagination.

" She will find out her mistake when she goes to speak to them an on the subject," I murmured; " but will she make any attempt to return the five hundred pounds to me? I doubt it. Well, it can't be helped."

I told Charlie all about the matter at lunch, and I was troubled to observe that he seemed to think it far more serious than I did.

"The man must have been humbugging you, I should think," he said, looking at me with an anxious pucker in his brows; "I can't see how it was possible for your mother to make such a mistake; why, all sorts of preliminaries would have to be gone through before a tradesman would accept such an order as that."

"That's possible," I replied; "but no doubt my mother doesn't understand that; you must remember she has never had the spending of large sums of money. What I imagine is, that she walked in, asked the price, said she should like a similar set, and left again under the impression the order had been accepted. She is awfully dictatorial, recollect."

"Well, but how about her address? Nobody could give such an order without leaving an address."

"Oh, I suppose she did leave her address," I replied, "for I remember Lucien said there was a carpet ordered there. That must be the explanation of it, Charlie, for I am certain the man spoke in good faith. Now it remains to be seen whether my mother will suggest returning any of the money. I am doubtful about it myself, though I wouldn't admit as much to any one but you."

"I am not doubtful about it," he said, looking at me in great perplexity.

Charlie was in the habit of making the best of my mother, and I was glad to hear him say this :

"You think she will return it, then ?"

"No, I do not," he answered grimly; "I am sure she won't."

After this there was a long silence between us, but presently Charlie rose and said impressively :

"Friend, you are a clever chap in many ways, but you have not the usual experience of a man of your years, and in some matters you are as simple as a child. Don't spend money on impulse, that's all, and consult the friends you know are true to you as often as you can."

He left the room quickly, but I noticed that after this he did not make the same excuses for my mother, in fact he avoided mentioning her name as much as possible, and constantly made inquiries as to my expenditure.

CHAPTER II.

THE end of July had come, and London was empty before my home was ready to receive me.

Charlie and I gripped each other hard by both hands, but neither of us spoke, when the moment for my departure from Wilton Crescent arrived; indeed our hearts were too heavy for words. No one can imagine the pang it cost me to separate from this dearly-loved friend, and I am afraid, in my selfish grief, the thought that Charlie would soon have a far dearer companion in my place, added to, rather than lessened, my sorrow.

But when I reached Brook Street, and in answer to my knock the door was imme-

diately thrown wide open, my spirits rose
considerably, and before I crossed the
threshold of the house my heart began to
beat with an unwonted sensation of pleasure.

I fancy in my nature there must be an
innate love of what some would call theatrical situations; any way, my mother's
arrangements for my reception at my new
home gave me a genuine thrill of enjoyment.

In the hall were marshalled the whole
of our household staff, five women servants and three men, and at the top of
the short flight of marble steps was my
mother herself, looking more dignified than
I could have imagined possible, in some
picturesque arrangement of black lace.

I stood for a moment gazing at the probably carefully-rehearsed scene, and then
my mother slowly descended the stairs,
saying in her clear, penetrating tones to
the smiling servants—

" Welcome your master, if you please."

At once they all bowed low, and I must
own a most unfamiliar flutter of pride

swept over me as I passed through the
obsequious little crowd and recognised the
fact that I was the master of this luxurious
house, and that all these people depended
upon me for their comfort and well being.

Before I entered the dining-room I had
time to form many good resolutions, and
to my inexpressible comfort I found that
the softness in my heart was reflected in
my mother's face; there was a troubled
look in her ordinarily hard, grey eyes, but
they rested on me with more tenderness
than I had seen in them yet.

"Mother," I said, clasping her hand in
mine and trying to steady my voice, for I
was ashamed to show her the strong emotion I felt, "it shall not be my fault if this
home is not a very happy one to you and
Lucien. I so earnestly desire to retrieve
my fault."

She looked into my eyes, and for a
moment I was almost alarmed at the extraordinary conflict of feeling I could read
in her face. It seemed to me that remorse

and fear of herself, as well as a curious, un-
willing tenderness, were plainly expressed in
her countenance. Her face and lips were
even paler than usual, her mouth twitched
nervously, and her hand trembled in mine.

These signs of weakness in this ada-
mantine woman, while they perplexed me,
touched me greatly.

"Mother," I murmured, putting my arm
round her, for I saw that she needed
support, "you are overwrought, the excitement has been too much for you.
Come, sit down quietly in your own easy
chair here by your own hearth."

But my words did not seem to bring her
any comfort; with a low moan she dis-
engaged herself from my arms, and stagger-
ing away sank into a chair by the table and
covered her scared face with her hands.

"What is it, what is it, mother?" I
cried, bending over her. "Come, tell me
your trouble; it grieves me that any
shadow should rest upon you to-day to
spoil your home-coming."

· "Stop, stop," she gasped, "don't speak to me for a minute; I shall be better by-and-bye; it is a passing attack of faintness, that is all."

And then, to my intense consternation, she broke down altogether, and, panting and struggling for breath, fell with her face upon her arms in a paroxysm of hard, dry sobs; such tearing, heart-breaking sobs as one hears from a man sometimes, but seldom from a woman.

"O, Friend, Friend," she wailed, "you are a good man, a good man; you deserve a better fate."

"Nay," I faltered, "God is merciful to me, inasmuch as he gives me an opportunity of making atonement to you. Do not grieve for me, mother, I am happier this moment than I ever thought to be, and do not lose hope on my account, for although it is long delayed, the day may come when my memory will return to me."

A strong convulsive shudder swept over

her, but her sobs ceased, and in another
minute she rose, having recovered her composure so completely that I own I was fairly
astonished.

"I am sorry," she said, with her usual
hard smile, "to have given you so cheerless
a welcome, my son; I intended that everything should be very bright. Well, you
must forgive me; it is not often that
I indulge in emotional displays of this
kind."

Her cold tones chilled me, but still this
little glimpse of what I believed to be her
real nature was a great consolation to me.
In her sorrow my heart had opened to my
mother for the first time.

"The time will come," I thought, "when
she will break through the barrier that is
between us." And then, under her escort,
I walked through the whole of my domain.

The rooms, with their rich, soft hangings
and draperies, splendid eastern carpets, and
artistic luxurious furniture, seemed to me
to be positively faultless from a home like

point of view. Even on this first day of occupation there was an air of having been used, and yet being in perfect order, about the whole place, that spoke volumes for the skill of the upholsterer who had planned the disposition of everything. Even the billiard-room, with the balls lying on the table, and a cue or two standing negligently about, seemed to speak of an interrupted game, while on the library table stood an open inkstand and blotting case.

" Does it please you ? " my mother asked at length.

" Entirely," I replied ; " and you, mother, are you satisfied ? "

" It is a little sombre, according to my notions," she responded, " but it is undoubtedly handsome."

We were in the spacious drawing-room at this moment, and I was obliged to turn my back upon her and walk away, that she might not perceive the amusement in my face as I contrasted the soft yellows and greys of the present hangings and furniture with the terrible glass-eyed parrots on their scarlet backgrounds.

As my eyes rested on this feast of pleasant subdued colour, which was agreeably relieved here and there by an oriental mat, an occasional chair, a flowering plant, or a piece of eastern embroidery of the brightest hues, my thoughts reverted in a spirit of real gratitude to my brother Lucien; but for his timely interference what might have been my sensations at this moment? In all probability, but for his hint, the whole thing would have been completed without any superintendence from me. I have a constitutional difficulty in dividing my attention, and having entrusted my mother with the furnishing of my home, my entire thoughts would have become engrossed by my business. The shock that my brother had saved me, therefore, really deserved the gratitude it won from me, and I reproached myself bitterly that I had not noticed his absence sooner.

"Why, where is Lucien?" I asked.

My mother looked at her watch, a small gold hunter with her monogram in diamonds on the back, with which I had presented her the previous day.

"He will be here in a few minutes," she said, "just in time to dress for dinner. You know his errand, don't you, Friend?"

"No," I replied, "I do not."

"Why, didn't you say Ella Maclise was to join us when we came to our new house?"

"Yes," I cried excitedly, "of course I did, but——"

"Well, then I would not let her remain one day longer in her situation than was necessary; I did not send for her while I remained at the Alexandra because I don't consider hotels quite suitable places for attractive young girls."

"Then, where is Lucien gone?" I asked

"To Euston Station to meet the Scotch express by which Ella travels, and which was due there five and twenty minutes ago."

A sound of wheels stopping outside the house interrupted her.

"Come," she said, "there they are, I expect; come and help me to welcome her."

I felt my cheeks flush, and I was glad that my mother had walked quickly on in front; but my heart beat high with pleasure, though I was conscious of a feeling of shyness which was quite new to me.

The door was opened when I arrived in the hall, and, standing rather in shadow, I saw my brother lead into the house so lovely a girl that I started in astonishment.

"Is it possible," I thought, "that this beautiful elegant woman can be that same fragile delicate child that I parted with only three years ago?"

At this moment, in greeting my mother, she turned her face towards me, and then I saw that it was the same, the very same, but grown so beautiful; so wonderfully, rarely beautiful !

The thin outlines had rounded, the pale

wan cheeks were wan no longer, a delicate pink flush mantled on them, and the wistful tender gray eyes sparkled with health and excitement.

Lost in admiration I gazed at her, while quietly and undemonstratively she thanked my mother for her welcome; but with my admiration there mingled an uneasy consciousness of regret, bitter unavailing regret.

" Would that she were less beautiful," I murmured to myself, " or that I were blind to it." And then I heard my mother say——

" And now, my dear, let me introduce you to my son. See, he is there, waiting to add his welcome to mine."

With a start the girl turned in the direction she indicated, and advanced towards me, but, until she was within a yard or two of where I stood with painfully beating heart, she did not raise her eyes. At this point, however, she looked up, and then with a quick cry of surprise she stopped short, gazing at me in the utmost perplexity and doubt.

Her confusion banished mine at once, and with outstretched hand I advanced to meet her.

"So you recognise me?" I said, taking her small gloved hand in mine. "Well, I am very glad that our paths of life have crossed each other. You won't reject my friendship now, will you?"

"Then it is you!" sho cried, clasping my hand in both of hers, her lovely eyes radiant with unaffected pleasure. "Oh, how glad I am! I have so often thought of your kindness to the poor forlorn little girl setting out to do battle with the great world. Oh, Mrs. Guadella, why didn't you tell me who Mr. Perditus was? If I had known that your son was that kind friend I have thought of so often, my impatience for this day would have been even greater."

In extreme astonishment my mother looked from one to the other of us, and, as she read in our countenances the joy that filled our hearts, a shadow came over her face, and a fierce gleam into her eyes.

"I don't understand," she muttered speaking thickly through her teeth, as she always did when annoyed. "Friend, why did you not tell me that you were already acquainted with Miss Maclise?"

"For this reason, mother," I said, terribly puzzled to find anything that sounded at all plausible, "I was not sure that Miss Maclise herself would wish to remember the circumstance. I am painfully aware of having acted with most outrageous want of ceremony on the only occasion I ever spoke to her, and I was by no means certain that she might not have a disagreeable recollection of me."

With this very lame explanation of what must have appeared most singular reticence on my part, I proceeded to tell my mother when and where I had met her *protegée* before, and I was thankful to her for accepting my excuses so readily.

The fact was I had never been able to

make up my mind to allude to our meeting,
for this reason: the strong interest this
young girl had inspired in me originated
in the intense sympathy I felt with her
for being in the society of the woman who
turned out to be my own mother. Had
my mother's appearance excited less aversion in me, it is just possible that her gentle
retiring girl companion would not have
enchained my attention at all at that time,
for three years before Ella Maclise was in
no way strikingly beautiful. It was the
sympathy I felt for her that made her so
interesting to me, and the reason for this
sympathy it was naturally quite impossible
to explain to my mother.

Miss Maclise was quick of perception,
and seeing that my mother was not too
well pleased at the open expression of our
gratification in meeting each other, with a
very sweet smile she turned away from me;
and declaring that she must go to her room
at once in order to render herself a little
en suite with the richness of her surround-

ings by dinner time, with a merry laugh
tripped up the stairs in the direction she
had seen her luggage carried.

Following her example, my mother, my
brother, and I repaired to our respective
apartments; and when our little party
re-assembled in the drawing-room, I thought
I had never seen a more charming picture
than Ella Maclise presented, as she stood
in her soft white silk gown against a background of green palm leaves and yellow
brocade.

My brother Lucien, in faultless evening
dress, the sombreness of which was relieved
by a glimpse of a dark crimson handkerchief thrust into his breast, leant over her,
evidently whispering something complimentary and pleasing, for there was an
arch smile on her full red lips; but I cannot say it afforded me any gratification to
recognise the fact that, under these circumstances, with a fine dusky colour in his
cheeks, his dark full eyes sparkling with
animation, and his small, black moustache

carefully waxed and turned up so as to leave his even white teeth and well-cut mouth fully exposed to view—my brother Lucien was by no means an unworthy companion for her.

I was standing some little distance apart, studying the couple with a grave face, I imagine, when a prodigious rustling of silks and jangling of ornaments interrupted my rather sad reverie. Looking up I saw my mother advancing towards me, her eyes ablaze with proud satisfaction.

For the moment I was simply thunderstruck with the gorgeousness of her attire, which is quite beyond me to describe, any further than that it was a sort of cloth of gold with raised crimson flowers upon it, and that a variety of ropes and strings of golden ornaments hung about it and jangled incessantly. Her shapely white arms were bare to the shoulder, and the corsage was—well—very much too *décolleté* to please me. Altogether, with her coal-black hair and gleaming eyes, my mother was painfully *prononcée,* and to turn from this glare and glitter to the simply-clad figure in the distance was a positive relief.

Fortunately for me my mother was quite satisfied with having so evidently surprised me. I imagine the idea that the impression created by her appearance could be an unfavourable one, did not come within the range of possibilities in her mind.

Walking to my side, she linked her arm in mine.

" Well," she said, following the direction of my eyes, " they are a well matched couple, are they not ? The very contrast of their complexions makes them an ex-cellent foil for each other."

Then, with a smile of conscious gratification she continued—

" I wish there were a few lookers-on to-night ; I think we are a most presentable quartette. You are a very well set up fellow, Friend, and I, well—— " with the smile intensified, " fine feathers make fine birds, eh, my son ? "

I had not the heart to damp her joy; after all, her pleasure was an innocent one.

"They are very fine feathers, indeed, mother," I replied smiling. "You positively took away my breath."

A little pang shot to my heart as I noticed the pleasure this very ambiguous compliment caused her; to me there is something piteous in the craving for personal admiration which one meets with occasionally in people whom nature has dealt very hardly with; this craving is an undoubted weakness, of course, for, after all, beauty alone makes neither man nor woman admirable or attractive; but which among us can afford to be severe on the weaknesses of another? In all probability, if we only knew ourselves, our own are so much more strongly marked that the term weaknesses would scarcely describe the very definite vanities and absurdities which exist within us.

"You really like my costume, then, Friend?" she murmured complacently.

"Well, mother," I replied, "it's a most wonderful get up."

"Yes, I flatter myself there is not another like it in London. As I said before, I wish we were not alone to-night."

I really could not re-echo this wish, for it occurred to me there was a faint chance that my mother might tire of her gorgeous gown before the autumn season arrived, and in that case she would probably find a considerable difficulty in procuring any material quite so *outre*, to replace it. After events proved, however, that I was mistaken in this; my mother really possessed a marvellous faculty for discovering combinations of colours in materials that I should never have thought could have been woven together in any Christian country. In comparison with some of the gowns she wore afterwards, the gold and crimson brocade was quiet.

The entry of the butler to announce that dinner was served was a relief to me. Re-

questing Lucien to conduct his companion,
I offered my arm to my mother, and,
preceded by the solemn, white-haired old
servitor, we marshalled into the dining-
room.

The appointments of the flower-decorated
table were faultless, the dinner and cooking
excellent. Being blessed with healthy ap-
petites we did justice to the good fare
provided for us, and when I raised my
glass and called to my companions to join
me in wishing all happiness to our family
party, quite a glow of hospitable pride and
pleasure filled my heart. It was really delightful to me to know that I was the giver
of the feast, and that to my exertions alone
those around me would owe the pleasure
and luxurious comfort they would enjoy in
the future.

As I say, this was a delightful moment
to me; but by far the happiest time of the
evening came when, after smoking a cigar
together, Lucien went out for a stroll, and I
repaired to the ladies boudoir, a charming

little room, in the tasty furnishing of which Gillow had surpassed himself.

Ella Maclise was alone when I entered, reclining in a pretty *crétonne*-covered chair; her delicate cheek was resting on her hand, and she was gazing dreamily in front of her, but when she became aware that I was in the room she sprang erect and came to meet me, her face suffused with blushes and her eyes glistening with emotion.

"Mr. Perditus," she said, "what can I say; how can I express to you the gratitude that fills my heart to-night?"

"Gratitude to me?" I stammered. "Oh, you mustn't say that; you are my mother's guest, remember. It is I who owe you a debt of gratitude for coming to grace our home with your presence."

She shook her head, but her eyes glistened more brightly still as she continued—

"Perhaps it would be more dignified of me to ignore the fact that you have anything to do with my present circumstances, but I cannot. It was very good of your mother to send for me again, but I know the truth; I know that however kindly her intentions were towards me she could not have rescued me from a very hard life of unappreciated drudgery but for your generosity. I can easily believe you do not desire my thanks, but I could not rest, indeed I could not, if I did not tell you to-night something of what I feel."

I took her hand in mine.

"You are under no obligation to me," I murmured, "pray remember that; it is my mother's doing entirely that you are here; but I thank God that he has given me the opportunity indirectly of being of service to you."

I was very much in earnest and very much moved, and I fancy there was something in my tone that startled her, for she withdrew her hand quickly, and when my mother entered a few minutes afterwards we were sitting quite quietly, lost in thought.

No sleep came to my eyes that night; in my mind there mingled such conflicting

sentiments of pain and pleasure that I was
well nigh distracted. At one moment I
lifted up my heart in thankfulness, and the
next, the recollection of my mother's words
with reference to Lucien's admiration for
the beautiful girl now slumbering beneath
my roof, plunged me into the deepest
despair.

But ere, with the morning light, I fell
asleep, I had argued myself into a calmer
condition. I had seen plainly that my
brother's admiration still continued,—indeed
how could it be otherwise?—and I resolved
to be true to him in word and deed; my
thoughts I could not answer for, but I determined to school even my thoughts with
the utmost diligence. I had injured Lucien
sufficiently in days gone by; in the future,
at least, he should have nothing to reproach
me with.

But, while it is within the bounds of
possibility to control our thoughts to some
extent, our dreams are entirely beyond our
influence, and, in the early morning hours of

the day which succeeded my home-coming, my dreams were full of Ella Maclise. Hand in hand with her I wandered under groves of trees, fairy-like in their sylvan beauty, and with her I floated on a moonlit sea.

My dreams were happy, perfectly happy, and when I awoke, although the sun shone gloriously and the birds outside the open window twittered blithely, I awoke with a sigh.

CHAPTER III.

LET it be clearly understood at once that this is no love story. In fact, it seems to me that stories on this subject, as they are generally written, are very unnatural things. How many a fictional love scene have we read, all of us? But what man or woman in real life ever repeated to another, even though that other were their mother or the chosen friend of their hearts, the words of love that have passed their lips, or fallen softly as the sweetest music on their enraptured ears?

In the strange incident of my life which forms the motive of this story there were no love scenes, and if there had been I should not venture to describe them. To me it appears a profanity to drag the pure love of a young girl into the garish light of publicity, and parade it, as it were. Moreover, I maintain that it is only fictional characters who ever do such things; and I have no hesitation in stating as a fact that a man or woman who would repeat the words of his or her lover would be shunned by all as a person of the lowest possible sensibilities.

Nevertheless, it must be stated that it was my misfortune at this time to fall hopelessly and completely in love: so much in love that one name was for ever trembling on my lips, one musical voice for ever rang in my ears, and one sweet face continually floated before my eyes.

When I awoke in the morning my first thought was of her; when I fell asleep at night I fell asleep repeating her name; there was not an instant in the day that I did not think of her. I loved the gown she wore; I worshipped the very ground she walked on, and many a time I have

E 2

kisssd the strings of the guitar which her taper fingers had pressed.

But I am glad to remember that throughout this period I never once swerved in my duty towards my brother, except so far as this. Although it tortured me, I could not deny myself the pleasure of thinking of my love, but I gave no outward sign of it. To Ella Maclise I was almost distant in my manner, but I hugged my secret to my breast, and many an hour I spent lost in blissful dreams of what might have been.

It was well for me that I was forced into business at this time, otherwise my passion might have proved too strong for me.

We did not leave town that year—we were too well pleased with our new home to wish to desert it at once; but in the long autumn evenings Ella and I would ride together, while Lucien was at the club to which Charles Hall had introduced him.

These evenings, we understood, were spent by my mother in practising her music. There was something mysterious about this singing of my mother's. I never could get her to perform before me, although I asked her very often to do so.

"No," she would always reply, "not yet, Friend. I am quite out of practice; I want you to hear me at my best when you do hear me. Have patience; at our house-warming I promise to surprise you."

Being really curious on this subject, I repeatedly questioned Ella and Lucien with regard to her vocal powers, but I never could arrive at any conclusion from their replies, beyond the fact that she possessed a fine voice, and had studied very diligently in her youth.

Smoothly and regularly our household seemed to work. The servants did their duty well, and everything was comfortable and orderly.

Before taking upon me the important position of head of a family, by Charlie Hall's advice I had consulted my good friends at Hampstead as to the course I

should pursue with regard to money, and
I remember being a little surprised by the
unanimity with which they responded to
my questions. It seemed to me as if they
must have talked the matter over among
themselves, so promptly they replied, and
so perfectly they agreed.

The result of our consultation was that I
was to draw a cheque on the first day of
each month for a certain sum, and that with
this sum the bills of the preceding month
were to be settled.

Mrs. Nesbit, whose father had been a man
of large property, was especially urgent with
regard to the desirability of monthly settlements with tradesmen. Curiously urgent, I
fancied, for as a rule she was by no means of
an argumentative turn of mind; and further-
more she and I had quite a battle of words as
to the amount of this monthly allowance. But
on this point I was firm, and added half as
much again to what she declared her mother
had considered a very liberal allowance to
maintain a far larger family than ours.

" I think you are foolish, Friend," she said at last, shaking her dear white head at me; " it is impossible that your mother could want as much as that for the household expenses."

" Well, then," I replied cheerfully, " there will be a little to spare—all the better. Don't you understand, dear old friend, that I want my mother to be absolutely free from anxieties. She won't be as good a manager as your mother was, therefore her money will not go as far. I don't want her to have to contrive and manage; in fact, I wish her to feel that she can have whatever she likes that is within reason."

" Well, any way, don't disregard my advice about the monthly payments," she said gravely.

" No," I replied, " I will not, indeed, and I thank you from my heart for all the interest you show in my affairs."

" It is a very sincere interest, Friend, depend upon that," she answered, rather wistfully; but for the rest of the evening she was very silent; and I should have gone away unhappy, fearing that I had offended her by my obstinacy, but for the warmth of her farewell.

Taking my face between her two soft palms, she pressed her lips upon my forehead.

"May your home be a very happy one, my dear," she said; "you deserve that it should."

The next morning I went the round of the tradesmen my mother and I had agreed to patronise. To each of them I explained my wishes; and I was a little surprised, considering the clamorous manner in which they had solicited our custom, at the perfect indifference they now showed whether they gave credit for one month or for six. At length, however, I managed to convince them that I was really in earnest, and then, with a decidedly condescending air, which proved how much I had fallen in their estimation by my very unfashionable proceeding, they consented to humour me in

my most unusual fancy for monthly reckon-
ings.

At the conclusion of the first month,
therefore, I gave my mother the specified
sum, and until the end of the second arrived
I never once thought of the matter again.

My brain indeed at this time was in a
curiously excited condition. When I had
leisure to think I was forced to acknowledge
that my circumstances were really and truly
very unhappy, and yet somehow I was conscious that I was not unhappy. I could not
be, when morning after morning Ella Maclise greeted me with her sweet sunny smile,
and when all day long as I sat in my city
office I could look forward to our meeting
when the day's work was over, and to our
quiet twilight canter.

Often I would try to rouse myself out of
this unreasonable state of content, and
would lay bare before my mind's eye the
most incontrovertible facts.

"She loves your brother; she is not for
you," I would murmur, and for the first

two months of our sojourn together I would reply, "I know it. I am only enjoying the present, where is the harm?"

But as the time went slowly on, and the days grew shorter and the solemn twilights longer, an undefined hope began to steal into my heart.

Granting that my brother loved Ella Maclise, and though his manner was scarcely that of a lover I had no reason to suppose that his sentiments towards her had altered, was it certain that she cared for him?

With this new doubt in my mind I watched her carefully, and an occasional thrill of joy would pass through me, as I noticed with what indifference she greeted him, and how bright her smile was when she turned her face to me. Still the thrill was by no means one of unalloyed happiness. If my brother loved her truly and fondly, it surely was my bounden duty to help him in that love, and with that perplexing harrowing thought in my mind I would receive her girlish kindness so coldly that oftentimes the fair cheek has flushed with mortification, its owner little recking that at that very moment I had hard work to prevent myself breaking into an open acknowledgment of my sentiments.

I saw little of my mother at this time; it was a grief to me that our tastes were so very dissimilar, but it was useless ignoring the fact that this was so, and that it was happier for both of us to meet as little as possible.

I will do her this justice, however; considering her nature she was curiously circumspect in her conduct and speech when Ella Maclise was present; in fact, the consideration she showed for her dependent guest raised her infinitely in my estimation; but when the girl was absent, as if freed from some crushing restraint, my mother would defy decorum to such a startling extent that I would positively shudder at the vehemence of her manner and expressions. At such signs

of confusion on my part she would openly
rejoice, and at these moments of unholy
delight she seemed positively demoniacal
to me.

The 28th of October, 1884, was the date
my mother had fixed for our formal house-
warming, and the 28th of October I shall
remember for many a long day.

To our house-warming every one that
we knew directly or indirectly had been
invited, for my mother even insisted,
despite my warm remonstrances, on in-
cluding on her cards of invitation the
friends of those who were themselves the
merest acquaintances.

" Why should I not do so, Friend ? " she
inquired with a hot gleam of anger in her
eyes. " I want to get into society, and
I don't care who knows it. I am no
humbug."

Ah, how slight an appreciation I had of
my mother's candour, and how often I
wished that she were more what she herself
would have called hypocritical; in fact it

would have pleased me far better for her to have assumed the virtue of conventional propriety in look and manner even if she had it not.

Personally therefore I was very much ashamed at the broadcast manner in which these invitations were sent out, and I must own that I was astonished when I found how readily almost without exception they were accepted.

Commenting on this fact, as, with Frank Nesbit, I sat by the familiar fireside at Wilton Crescent, to which Charlie had just returned after a month on the Continent with his sweet bride, my remarks were received with an outburst of laughter from the irrepressible Frank.

"You are surprised, are you, my boy? Why, good gracious me, man, people are positively dying to get inside your house. You must remember, 'You are a funny family, you are, you are, you are!'"

"What do you mean?" I cried, not too well pleased.

Throwing himself back in his chair, heedless of his pretty sister's little frowns and *moues*, Frank laughed until his bald head even grew flushed.

"Oh, Lord, Perditus!" he gasped. "I never came near a fellow with so small an idea of a joke as you; that's what makes you such a splendid companion, you take everything so delightfully seriously. Oh, hang it, Julia, stop those nods, and becks, and wreathed smiles. I shall die if I don't laugh, and you had better have a cross friend in your house than a defunct brother, any day."

"I am not cross," I said, so ungraciously that Frank roared louder than ever; "but I don't understand you."

"He means," explained Charlie, who could scarcely keep from smiling himself, "that people are curious about you, Friend. Oh, shut up, Frank, there's no hearing oneself speak."

"Why should they be curious?" I asked uneasily.

"Why, don't you see, old fellow," my good friend continued gently, "your strange story has got buzzed about somehow, and you know your mother is——"

"Is what?" I asked gloomily.

"Well, she has made herself rather conspicuous. Any way, people want to find out what you are all like."

"Well, I hope we shall answer their expectations. We are certainly eccentric."

Which bitter speech on my part afforded Frank Nesbit, whose genuine love of teasing was rather at variance with his exceedingly soft nature, unmixed pleasure.

Julia Hall, however, restored me to something like equanimity before I left.

"Don't mind him, Friend," she said, laying a kind hand on my arm, "he can't help chaffing; but there's no man in London he respects and loves so well as you, except Charlie, and mother and I agree with him in that, as we agree with him in everything, bless his dear, aggravating old heart."

"Don't you be afraid of the criticisms of

society," she continued soothingly. "I defy
any one to find fault with you, Friend,
when you try to make yourself agreeable.
Your brother, too, is very pleasant, while as
for Ella Maclise, well, I don't know a
prettier or more charming girl."

But when she had said this she grew
painfully confused, and I was perfectly
aware that her embarrassment arose from
the consciousness of being unable to say
one word in approval of my mother, certainly the principal figure in our family
quartette.

CHAPTER IV.

On the 28th of October I arose in a very depressed state of mind. I dreaded the evening, and the responsibilities that would attach to me as host on the occasion. Under any circumstances I should have felt these responsibilities a heavy burden, but I could not ignore the fact that my mother's eccentricities, and the painful uncertainty of how she would comport herself, were the principal causes of my anxiety.

I was depressed on this particular morning also for another reason. Four days previously I had given my mother the third of my monthly cheques, and 1 could not help noticing that she had received it in rather a curious manner.

She had said nothing on the occasion, but immediately I placed the slip in her hand, without a word she had walked out of the room quickly, and when in some surprise I turned to Lucien to seek an explanation of her peculiar manner, I had seen that an almost ghastly pallor overspread his face, and that his hand trembled, as with affected indifference he stroked his small silky moustache.

After this I could not shut my eyes to the fact that my mother and brother avoided being left alone with me, and the night before the morning of which I speak this avoidance had been so marked that I had retired to rest seriously uneasy.

My gloomy sensations, however, were dispelled before I reached the breakfast-room. As I passed the drawing room the sweet voice that always sent a thrill through me called my name. I entered, and then stopped short with an involuntary exclamation of admiration.

At first sight the floor seemed covered

with a wealth of fragrant blossoms, and, kneeling in the midst of the choice exotics and delicate roses, herself a fairer flower than any there, was Ella Maclise, with a large white apron on and sleeves turned up to the elbow.

"There," she said, "don't come any nearer, Mr. Perditus, or you will tread upon them. I wanted you to see them just as they came from the market. Are they not lovely?"

"They are, indeed!" I replied fervently, looking her straight in the eyes.

My words were painfully commonplace. I wonder was there ever a man in such a situation before, who missed so palpable an opportunity of saying something pretty; but though my words indicated little I imagine my expression must have been very eloquent, for Ella's cheek flushed under my open admiration, and busying herself among the flowers, she continued quickly—

"I must ask you to make my excuses to Mrs. Guadella this morning, Mr. Perditus."

" Your excuses, for what ? "

" For absenting myself from breakfast."

" Why, are you not well, this morning ? "

" Oh, very well," she answered merrily. " In fact so well that I had an appetite an hour and a half ago. I_breakfasted while you were still asleep, I suspect."

" But what made you do that? " I cried disappointedly, for I felt that our meal would be a very dismal one without her.

"Why, I coaxed Mrs. Guadella into allowing me the entire superintendence of the floral decorations for our party, instead of entrusting them to the Convent Garden florist, and I assure you, with two maids to help me, I shall not get the flowers arranged any too soon to prevent their withering."

" But it is so much for you to do," I murmured, gazing at the masses of bloom that lay around her. " You will be so tired."

" Indeed I shall not," she replied, smiling up at me. " Mr. Perditus, I have posi-

tively looked forward to this morning. I
have been dreadfully lazy lately, and I am
quite thankful for some occupation. Do
you know, when the excitement of this
reception is off our minds, I have a scheme
in my head which I hope to carry out, with
your assistance? "

"What is that?" I asked.

"Why, I want you to persuade your
friend, Mrs. Charles Hall, to let me help
her in her work among the poor. I felt
quite guilty the other day when her husband
was speaking with such enthusiasm of her
labours of love. The only excuse I can
make for myself is that I wanted a little
holiday after my three years of drudgery.
However, now I am thoroughly rested, and
I mean to put my shoulder to the wheel in
good earnest, when, as I say, the anxiety of
to-night is over."

"The anxiety of to-night, you may well
call it," I said gloomily. "I would give
a thousand pounds willingly to get out of
the whole thing."

With a quick look of sympathy she glanced up at me, but she lowered her eyes immediately, and feigned to be busily occupied with her flowers, as she replied,—

"Don't worry yourself unnecessarily. I can't bear to see your face so anxious; you do so much to make others happy, it seems hard that you should be less comfortable yourself."

"Forgive me for what I am going to say, Mr. Perditus," she continued nervously, "but I wish, I really wish, that you were not so sensitive as to the opinion of others. So long as we do what is right, let people think what they choose, it doesn't appear to me to matter much whether they admire us or not. Come, cheer up; the evening will go off well, I have no doubt; at any rate, if we all do our best to make it a success we can do no more."

Ella Maclise was right, but though I recognised the wisdom of her words I could not argue myself into anything like a philosophical frame of mind as to the verdict of society upon my family and myself. We all know that very young people suffer real misery when they imagine that some eccentricity, either in themselves or their companions, brings them into ridiculous prominence. It is quite useless to tell a girl or a lad that such and such a social solecism, which appears to them terribly flagrant and glaring, will not be noticed; they have not the capability of grasping this undoubted fact; and I think elder people display great selfishness in ignoring this sensitiveness as they do. Surely they cannot as a rule have forgotten so completely the days of their own youth, and the agonies they suffered when father or mother, or uncle or aunt, would insist upon doing something, or wearing something, which seemed in their inexperienced eyes to be horribly "bad form."

Don't let it be imagined that I think the young people are in the right when they fancy mother's shawl, or father's inconvenient habit of taking snuff at important points, will rivet the attention of an entire

theatre. I know that in reality these objectionable garments and habits will attract no
attention whatever, but I argue from this
point—until you can convince your lads and
lassies that this is so—and it appears to me
that elder people never try to convince them
—it is cruel to inflict these petty punish-
ments upon them. Young people are not
wise, that is an acknowledged fact, but who
would wish them to be so ?

Therefore I maintain that " crabbed age "
should do its best to make itself agreeable
to " golden youth," since but for the brightness of golden youth our closing days would
be dull indeed.

In years of course I had long passed this
period of acute self-consciousness, but the
singularity of my condition was in nothing
more strongly exemplified than in this. I
was able to recognise and be ashamed of my
own over sensitiveness, but perhaps it was
even emphasized on this very account.

My mother and Lucien were seated at the
breakfast table when I entered ; but before

she greeted me my mother rose hastily and, pulling the bell violently, desired the servant to summon Miss Maclise immediately. I could not fail to notice the excitement of her manner, nor that my brother also was very ill at ease.

" It's no use sending for Miss Maclise, mother," I said quietly, looking in some surprise at half a dozen letters that lay upon my plate, for even now I had few private correspondents.

" Why not ? " she cried harshly.

" She has had her breakfast. She told me to ask you to excuse her; she is arranging the flowers."

" But I will not excuse her. Go up, John, and tell Miss Maclise I must request her to come down at once."

But the man had scarcely left the room before an expression of astonishment broke from my lips, and, running to the door, I countermanded my mother's order. I had opened one of my letters, and at a glance I had read these words—

"Sir,—As I told you, I did not care whether your account ran for six or even twelve months, but you were very firm in wishing monthly settlements. Under these circumstances, therefore, I am not prepared to give you longer credit; and, as the three monthly accounts I sent in were unusually heavy ones, I must decline supplying you any further without receiving a cheque. These three accounts amount to £300, and I should be glad to receive this sum at your convenience."

"What do you mean, Friend, by disputing my wishes?" cried my mother, with a very sorry assumption of confidence.

"I will tell you in a minute," I replied grimly; "it is not quite correct, I believe, to discuss money matters before your guests."

With which I tore open the other notes. As I expected they were from five other tradesmen, and were, like the first, demands for an immediate settlement of their claims, which amounted—the six together—to the very considerable sum of eleven hundred pounds. What then had become of the money I had given to my mother in three separate cheques of five hundred pounds? Out of this all the tradesmen's bills were to have been paid, as well as the servants' wages, which last I shrewdly suspected were also in abeyance.

One after another I read the letters through, and, as I laid the last down, my mother rose as if to leave the room.

"Do not go," I said, endeavouring to restrain the anger I felt. "I must understand the meaning of this."

"The meaning of what?" she asked, with a ghastly attempt at bravado.

"Of these notes. They are all demands for money."

"Oh, they have written to you, have they? I did not think they would do that, although they threatened it. Well, they will find they have been fools, for they have lost a good customer through it."

"Do you really mean to tell me," I cried

sternly, for her flippant, defiant manner
irritated me past endurance, "that I really
owe this large sum of money?"

"Certainly you do, and another hundred
added to that for servant's wages."

I literally gasped with astonishment.

"Then you have paid nothing—absolutely nothing?"

"No, I have not," she replied, with a
dogged frown.

"But where is the fifteen hundred pounds
I gave you for that purpose?"

She looked me boldly in the face. By
this time she was far the cooler of the two.

"Where is the fifteen hundred pounds?"
she repeated calmly. "Well, I don't desire
to mystify you in any way, my son. The
facts of the case are these: I do not
approve of monthly settlements with tradesmen; they never respect people who pay
them too readily; and, moreover," she continued, with indescribable malice, "I did
not choose to be dictated to by Mrs. Nesbit
at second-hand."

I started, and my mother went on with a sneering laugh :

"Why, my son, you don't suppose I am such a fool as not to recognise Mrs. Nesbit's prudence in your household wisdom. Well, I was not going to let your revered old friend rule me, so I determined at once to manage my own house in my own way, and to have quarterly instead of monthly payments."

I drew a deep breath of relief. After all, if my mother suspected that I had acted on Mrs. Nesbit's advice, perhaps her irritation and obstinacy were not very unnatural, for I had noticed several times that though she displayed no tenderness towards me herself, a word from me of appreciation for my dear old friend excited a strong feeling of angry jealousy in her. For this reason I had, I fancied, very carefully concealed the fact of my consultation with the Hampstead friends, but not being clever at subterfuge I must have let it slip out in some unguarded moment.

"I am sorry, mother," I said gently, "that we do not think alike on this subject, and also that you should fancy I wished to hamper you or dispute your authority in your own home. In future it shall be as you desire, and I will give you the cheques every three months if you think it will be better. After all," I continued, trying to speak cheerfully, "there is no great harm done, except that it is unpleasant to receive such notes as these; but if you will give me the money I will go and settle with these persons, and explain to them how we wish it to be in the future."

Deliberately she brushed the crumbs off her lap, and then, throwing herself into an easy chair, she leant back in her favourite attitude, and looked up into my face with the most perfect composure. For a moment she stared at my perplexed countenance, and then she burst into a fit of harsh, repulsive merriment.

In great uneasiness I waited for her to recover her gravity, for I knew by painful experience that nothing awoke my mother's sense of humour except the mortification or discomfort of another.

A minute or two, sitting at her ease protecting her face from the fire with a gorgeous hand-screen, my mother continued to laugh, and then, stopping abruptly, she said :

"Friend, what do you suppose is amusing me ? "

" I cannot say," I replied shortly, "and I should be glad, mother, if you would be serious ; I feel far from merry myself this morning."

"There's no occasion to tell me that, my son ; you are in an awful funk, I can see that from your face. Why, your solemn pragmatical countenance would make a cat laugh, I do believe. But your face is not the only funny thing about you."

With an impatient gesture I thrust my hands into my pockets and began pacing up and down the room.

" Come, mother," Lucien interposed in a

very faltering tone, "explain what you mean to Friend; I don't see the use of teasing him in this way."

"Don't you?" replied our mother calmly. "Oh, you are an ass, Lucien, we all know that. I shall treat your brother exactly as I choose, and you too, for the matter of that."

Thoroughly roused, I stopped in front of her.

"Mother," I said, "let there be no more of this; give me the money and let me go."

The sneering smile on her lips never altered, but her fierce eyes quailed for an instant under mine, and she shifted uneasily in her chair.

"Why, my dear son," she said, "it's your very confidence that you will get the money back that amuses me so. It's very complimentary, of course, but it's a little simple of you, too."

Hopelessly mystified I stood gazing down at the crafty, cruel, smiling face.

" I don't understand you," I murmured.

Rising, she drew herself to her full height
and faced me boldly.

" Then I will speak plainly. I can't
give you back the money, for I have
spent it."

" You have spent fifteen hundred
pounds ! "

" Yes, fifteen hundred pounds exactly."

" But on what, in the name of wonder ? "

" On diamonds," she replied, looking me
straight in the eyes.

I sank into a chair by the side of the
table and leant my aching head upon my
hand. My brain felt confused and dizzy,
and a sensation of hopeless depression was
upon me.

" On diamonds ? " I repeated blankly.

" Yes, on diamonds."

" But why didn't you tell me ? " I said,
trying to shake off the heavy weight that
lay upon my spirits.

" Because I only made up my mind to
buy them the day before yesterday. A

man Lucien knows told him of them, and I determined to secure them if I could for our 'at home.' It would have been a little discreditable to you, Friend, if your mother had appeared on such an occasion without jewellery."

"But why use that money? Why not have explained the matter to me? I have not denied you anything yet, mother," I said sadly.

"Well, you are making a pretty fuss about this, at any rate. I meant to tell you at my own time, and that would have been to-night after the party. I wanted you to see the jewels before you heard about them. Upon my soul, Friend Perditus, you are very much mistaken if you think I am going to put up with lectures from my own son. I told you six months ago that I should require jewellery this winter, and I wasn't going to let a bargain like this escape me. Why, after all, what is fifteen hundred pounds to you? When all is paid we don't live anywhere near up to your income."

What could I say? It was true, this fifteen hundred pounds was not a serious loss to me, and, God knows, regret for the money had no place in my harrassed mind. What pained me so inexpressibly was the thought of my mother's want of honour; for my eyes were wide open now; she could not deceive me any longer; I knew that from the first she had been appropriating this money to her own purposes, and would have continued to do so until my debts had assumed really formidable proportions, had not the tradesmen taken the matter into their own hands.

With a very heavy heart I rose, and going into the library rang the bell; the butler answered it, and through him one by one the servants were sent to me. Before I left the house, carrying in my pocket-book a separate cheque for each tradesman, the wages were settled in full and the servants informed that on each quarter day, at the same hour, and in the same place, their claims would be satisfied.

I was drearily conscious that my mother would violently resent this act on my part as being calculated, as in fact it was, to undermine her authority in her own house; but I could not help that; one of two things was inevitable, and since the relations between us were already so strained, I preferred to incur her displeasure still further, rather than live under a burden of debt.

As I was crossing the hall with my hat on, Lucien came out of the dining-room, and, carefully closing the door behind him, placed his hand on my arm.

" Friend," he whispered nervously, " I am very sorry for what has happened. I tried in vain to convince my mother that she ought to speak to you before purchasing the jewels, but she positively refused to do so. I hope you will not blame me in the matter."

"I don't wish to blame any one," I replied very wearily. "I am sorry my mother has so little confidence in my desire to give her pleasure, but since it is so I must bear it as well as I can. Don't you worry yourself, Lucien," I continued more kindly, "at least there need be no coolness between us over this unfortunate misunderstanding."

I stretched out my hand and clasped his even more warmly than I had intended, for his pale cheek had flushed at my words, and his eyes were full of shame.

CHAPTER V

But though my brother's sympathy to some extent consoled me, I spent a very miserable day. My interviews with the tradesmen were far from pleasant. One and all they had grievances against my mother, to which grievances I was forced to listen, sorely against my will; and when I had transacted this business there was nothing left me but to repair to the club. I had stated my intention of absenting myself from the city the day before, and I did not wish to gain a character for whimsicality among my clerks; neither did I think it desirable to go home until it was absolutely necessary. I was sure my mother would not wish my society, and this sentiment I echoed most heartily.

It was nine o'clock when I returned to my house, and the hall and stairs were already illuminated with numberless coloured lamps, which twinkled among the leaves of palms and tropical plants of all kinds. It was a pretty, cheery scene, and my spirits revived slightly under the influence of the light and brightness, but as I passed my mother's room they dropped again like lead.

Each of the bed rooms was provided with double doors, but even these could not soften the harsh tones of my mother's voice; and I heard her rating her maid with ungovernable fury.

Scarcely had I passed than the door flew open, and the French lady's-maid emerged, with flashing eyes.

"Sir," she said, hastening after me, "let it be plainly understood, I will not dress madame or attend to her ever again. She has struck me. If I did not feel for you great respect and pity—yes, pity, sir—I would appeal in the court of law against madame. As it is, I say good-bye to your house within one hour."

How my mother would accomplish her toilette I failed to imagine; but I gathered afterwards that she called in the services of Ella Maclise, for the girl's sweet face was flushed, and there was an anxious pucker between the brows when she descended to the drawing-room, which anxiety I was certain had nothing to do with her own toilette, which was entirely charming, but, as usual, perfectly simple. If I had had any doubts, her first words would have dispelled them.

"Mrs. Guadella will be down in a few minutes," she said. "I am sorry that Hortense has vexed her. I was afraid we should never be ready. The invitations were for ten, and, listen, there is half-past striking. Fortunately, nobody is punctual on these occasions."

"I thought I heard a row," said Lucien

coolly. "So you have been lady's-maid, I suppose, Ella ?"

"Yes, I did what I could; but I can't replace Hortense, and I am afraid your mother found me very awkward; any way, she seemed anxious to dismiss me. Well, what do you think of the decorations ?"

"Delightful!" we both exclaimed heartily; and then, with a little cry of—

"Oh, I had nearly forgotten!" she ran away and left us.

"I am sorry, in more ways than one, that mother should have quarrelled with Hortense to-night," Lucien commenced gloomily.

"Why, you mean that she was already ruffled, I suppose ?"

"No, that's not exactly what I mean. I am sorry because Hortense was a very wholesome check upon mother."

"In what way ?"

"Why, in the matter of complexion. Oh, upon my soul, Friend, you are very dense in some respects. You must know by this time that mother touches up very extensively. Well, without Hortense to superintend matters, I am rather afraid the result will be a little too strong for some of our friends. However, for goodness sake appear to shut your eyes to it, whatever it is. Don't get deeper into mother's black books, if you can help it."

In a fever of uneasiness I awaited her appearance, and I am afraid the delicate button-hole, which Ella had carefully prepared for me as well as for Lucien, was not received in the gracious spirit it merited.

But though my anticipations with regard to my mother were sufficiently dismal, they did not at all prepare me for the reality.

Never shall I forget the livid pallor of her face, thickly covered with a horrible blueish white powder, which rendered her dark cavernous nostrils and ghastly lips more conspicuous than ever; her eyebrows and eyelashes, too, were loaded with black

cosmetic, and altogether, in a gown of
rank green satin and gold, with a flaring
necklace of what appeared to me to be very
questionable diamonds, my mother presented
so horrible an aspect that I really felt, at
the risk of enraging her, I positively must
remonstrate, and beg her at least to remove
the terrible paint, which made her face,
at all times forbidding, almost diabolical
in its ugliness.

I was further urged to take this course
when I saw the involuntary blush of shame
which suffused the cheek of the fair girl
who stood looking timidly on. Firmly I
advanced to my mother, and, laying my
gloved hand upon her arm, I whispered—

"Mother, I don't want to annoy you,
but I must beg a favour from you."

With an impatient gesture she shook my
hand off, and turned her bloodshot eyes on
my face.

"Don't ask me any favour, Friend,"
she said aloud in harsh tones. "I have

been very much upset, and you had better leave me alone, unless you want to hear a bit of my mind before our guests."

"But I must speak," I said, "before any one comes. Mother, for Heaven's sake take some of that horrible stuff off your face, you can have no idea how conspicuous it is in this strong light."

For an instant I thought she would have struck me, and in alarm I stepped quickly backwards; but this unconcealed trepidation on my part restored her equanimity at once; the lurid gleam of rage died out of her eyes, and placing her hands on her hips she threw her head back and laughed until I felt the beads of perspiration start upon my brow.

She was still laughing when the first knock resounded through the house, and then Lucien, running to her, seized her arm and shook it violently.

"Stop, mother," he cried furiously, "for mercy's sake stop that hateful noise, and behave decently, if you can."

To my astonishment the harsh discordant sounds died away as if by magic, and the tiger-like eyes grew almost soft as they rested on my brother.

" Don't speak so angrily, Lucien," she murmured. " I will do anything you ask."

And then the first guest entered, and for the next hour I was so fully occupied greeting each fresh arrival that I had absolutely no time to think on any subject.

At length, however, there came a cessation in the continuous string of announcements and then, with a young girl of my acquaintance, the daughter of Charlie's oldest patient, who was making her *début* into society on this occasion, I strolled through the rooms into the illuminated conservatory, from which we could hear the music though we could not see the performers.

Wearily I listened to a long violin solo, while, wondering uneasily what they thought of us, I watched the elegantly dressed throng who crowded my rooms almost to suffocation; and very grateful I felt to my young companion for so pleasantly chatting away about the beauty of the decorations, and her delight at being "out," as though I had been a thoroughly satisfactory and sympathetic listener, instead of a moody man out of humour with himself and with all the world.

The violin solo was received in a spirit of perfect good breeding—that is to say, very coldly and indifferently—and then followed a bravura tenor song, which also was put up with civilly by the listeners. On the termination of this song, however, we noticed, even from where we sat, a great stir and flutter of excitement among the guests.

"What's going to be done now?" asked the young girl by my side.

"I am sure I don't know," I answered, smiling down at her eager face; "I don't think there is a printed programme, and I have had nothing to do with the musical arrangements."

At this moment a soft clapping of hands interrupted me.

"This is somebody important, I should fancy," I began, and then I stopped as a shrieking soprano note—of such an ear-piercing quality that involuntarily I shook my head with a little shiver—rang through the rooms.

"Good gracious!" cried my companion, with a girlish giggle, "that took away my breath, as it did yours, Mr. Perditus; and look at all the people round—there is scarcely one that can keep their countenances. How they are crowding forward. Oh, please take me into the other room, Mr. Perditus; I want to see this quite too utterly intense singer."

"It's one of the Opera people, I imagine," I said, as with difficulty I slowly penetrated the throng; "my mother said she had engaged one or two of the Opera-house artistes, but I think she has made a mistake in her selection in this case."

Here our progress was hindered by a

young couple, who, arm-in-arm, stood directly in our path, and were talking so earnestly that they did not hear my whispered request that they would let us pass. On the other hand, however, every word they spoke was audible to my companion and me.

"Oh, Fred," said the girl, "don't laugh—she's absolutely awful."

"Not a bit of it," was the reply; "I think she's jolly fun! I wouldn't have missed this for fifty pounds. It's really magnificent catawauling."

Here, interrupted by a more than usually piercing note, the young man stopped abruptly, and holding his handkerchief to his mouth, his shoulders began to heave with unrestrained mirth. But his partner did not share his merriment.

"I really wish you wouldn't laugh, Fred," she pleaded; "I feel very uncomfortable—she's so dreadful—and it is such a pity, for the others are so nice."

Finding I could not attract their attention, I touched the young man lightly on the arm. But there was no need for me to speak. When his eyes encountered mine, with a smothered exclamation he drew aside hastily, and, glancing up at him to return my thanks, I saw that his face was scarlet to the very brow, and that altogether he was in a state of pitiable confusion.

Smiling down at the merry girlish face by my side, I said with mock intensity—

" Now you know what a man looks like when he is detected in the act of committing some horrible crime. Did you ever see a more guilty object than that ? "

" Poor fellow," my companion replied, with a smothered giggle, " I am really sorry for him, but he is old enough to be more careful. If I fell into the mistake of criticising the entertainment that was offered me without being sure who was behind me, no one need be surprised, for I am only just out of my shell you know. By-the-bye, Mr. Perditus," she continued very gravely, " perhaps after all I had better not try to get a sight of this remarkable singer of yours, for if she is funny I am bound to laugh—I can't help it really—and then I may offend you."

"You needn't be afraid," I said; "you may laugh as much as you like, you won't hurt my feelings——" and then suddenly I came to an abrupt stop.

By this time we had reached the edge of the circle, in the midst of which the shrieking singer stood, but before I had turned my eyes in her direction I felt my arm violently clutched, and then, to my extreme surprise, my girl companion loosened her grasp; and ere I could seek any explanation of her extraordinary behaviour I saw her, with bent head and crimson cheeks, pushing her way through the laughing crowd at my back, whose mocking eyes were steadily fixed on one centre of attraction.

"What in the world is the matter with her," I thought, as I prepared to follow her. "Is the room too hot, or does she find this yelling a little too much at close quarters? She may well do so."

Here I turned my head to take a hasty

glance at the singer before I also beat a
retreat, but if I wished to rejoin my companion, it would have been wiser to withdraw in happy ignorance of who the singer
was who was so evidently an object of
derision to all my guests ; for, no sooner had
my eyes fallen upon the figure which stood
in front of the piano, than all power of
movement forsook me ; and, as if comatosed
by the deadly fascination of a snake, I
remained spellbound gazing upon the de-
grading spectacle.

It was my mother who stood there, with
her coarse mouth distended, her head
thrown back. and her glassy, glittering eyes
—which reflected the lights of the chandelier
above her —fixed with an unearthly expression of tragic intensity on a distant point of
the room. Her thick heavy brows were
contracted until they nearly met above the
flat broad nose, while the tightly-drawn-
back lips — whose livid purple hue was
indescribably horrible contrasted with the
absolute deathly ghastliness of the face—

disclosed the large white teeth, which appeared to be the fringe of a black yawning cavern. Her arms were bare to the shoulder, and while she sang she flung them about in the most frenzied of gesticulations. Now the hands would be outstretched above the head in agonised pleading, and then clasped tightly upon her heaving bosom ; while her portly figure, in utter abandonment, swayed to and fro and seemed to writhe with theatrical musical fervour.

Whether from a musical point of view my mother's was a creditable performance or not I cannot say, I only know that I am powerless to convey any notion of the agony of shame which I suffered then.

With lowered eyes and beating heart I stood there until the end of the passionate operatic love song, and I think I never experienced a greater sensation of relief than when the last moaning note died away, and— apparently utterly exhausted by her emotional exertions—my mother sank into a chair which had been placed by the side of the piano, and pressing both hands over her heart, nodded her head solemnly in response to the burst of ironical applause which thundered through the crowded room.

"I will speak to Lucien at once," I thought , dabbing my moist forehead with my handkerchief; "he must and shall prevent a recurrence of this."

But ere I had moved a yard my steps were arrested again.

An excited little Italian of a most loathsome, greasy, dirty appearance, darted to my mother's side, and, seizing her hand in his, cried—

"Bravo, madame! Bravo! A thousand thanks! Now another, another! Show your friends the extent of your surpassing talent. Sing a duet with me, or, better still, one of your own French chansonettes."

This proposal was received with acclamations on all sides, and, baffled and miserable, I gave up the struggle in despair.

With a ghastly smile of gratified vanity my mother rose again, and with a whispered observation to Lucien, who I now perceived was seated at the piano, she struck an attitude and commenced the French chansonnettte.

Five minutes before I should have said my mortification was so complete that nothing could add to it; but the first stanza of my mother's little song showed me my error. Her impassioned fervour was hard enough to bear, but in comparison with her arch smiles and heavy repulsive coquetry it was an elevating exhibition.

One verse I endured, and then, sick at heart, I turned away, and unceremoniously pushed my way through my guests, who were taking advantage of the song's being of a light character to indulge their hitherto suppressed mirth openly.

On the outskirts of the crowd I encountered Charlie Hall and his wife and mother-in-law. The old lady, whose bright eyes were dim with sympathy, came up to me at once, and I noticed that her hand shook as she pressed mine warmly.

"We are going now, Friend," she faltered.

"What already?" I said gloomily. "Well, I am not surprised."

"Julia feels the heat rather too much for her," Charlie interposed quickly, "so Frank has gone to look for the carriage. Make our excuses to your mother, there's a good fellow."

Then laying a hand upon my arm he continued—

"Friend, come round to me, when this is all over, and stay the night. I'll sit up for you, and we'll have a smoke and a chat as we did in the old days."

The tears rose to my eyes, and I turned my head quickly away. I understood him so fully; he knew how sore my heart was, and he also knew how dear his sympathy was to me. I wrung his hand hard in mine, but I answered—

"I cannot come, Charlie, there are some things that I must do to-night before I go to rest."

Seeing that I was resolved, he did not attempt to persuade me, but the two women looked very wistfully at me when they bade me farewell; and even Frank Nesbit was grave for once as, taking me by the arm, he drew me apart from the rest, and whispered—

" Perditus, old man, don't be offended, but I should feel myself unfriendly if I didn't tell you one thing. Give your mother some real diamonds, my boy. It is natural for women to like glitter, but it doesn't look well for your mother to be wearing such outrageous shams as those. I have heard a hundred people speak of them. I shouldn't have mentioned it, Friend, if I hadn't known how innocent you are in these matters. Good-bye, old man, now don't make a mountain out of this molehill to-night."

With that he handed his own reverend, dignified old mother down the steps, and I thought bitterly how different his sensations would have been could he have changed places with me at that moment.

CHAPTER VI

THE rest of that miserable evening I will not attempt to describe. Indeed at all an adequate description would be quite beyond my power, of how my mother's excitement grew and grew, of how she sang again and again, finishing up after supper with a characteristic duet from a French opera bouffe, in which the objectionable vulgar little Italian tenor assisted her.

I imagine, in another way, my conduct must have been as eccentric and possibly as blameworthy as my mother's; for, utterly crushed, I made no attempt to amuse my guests, partly through sheer inability, and partly because I was bitterly conscious that they were already brimming over with

merriment at the expense of my household
without any effort on my part.

At last, however, the specified hour for
the close of our "at home" having arrived,
the guests departed quickly.

At a quarter past two the rooms were
empty, except for ourselves; and then,
humming the refrain of the opera bouffe
duet, my mother flung herself into a lounge,
and, as usual, crossed her feet in front of
her.

"Fetch me a brandy-and-soda, Lucien,"
she said, "that scene of Planquette's makes
one's throat dry, I can tell you. Why,
where's Maroni? I told the little chap to
wait and have a drink after the others were
gone. It's a long while since we've sung
together, and he's as full of spirits and go
as an egg's full of meat. Just look for him,
Lucien, and say I want him."

"Lucien need not trouble, mother," I
interposed curtly. "Signor Maroni has
gone."

"Gone?" she exclaimed.

" Yes, I told him you were fatigued."

" Oh, that's all rubbish," she said, with a savage glitter in her eyes. " I wish you wouldn't interfere, Friend. The little man was dry; he told me so, and considerably astonished old Lady Parkinson, who was saying good-bye at the time, by doing so. It's too bad. All the pubs will be shut by this time, and I promised him a good draught. I don't suppose he's got a drop of anything at home; he's as poor as a church mouse, and I wanted you to give him a ten pound note, too. He really must have a more decent coat before he comes again. However, he will turn up to-morrow, I have no doubt. I told him there would always be a knife and fork at our table for him, and by the way he punished the supper," continued my mother, with her ghastly laugh, " I should say that eating has not been much in his line lately. You should have seen Lady Marie Hazlitt stare at him ; I roared with laughter."

Uneasily Lucien approached me. I imagine

he saw a determination to speak in my face.

"Friend," he whispered, "don't argue with mother to-night. I know her better than you do. She is over-excited, what with one thing and another," he continued meaningly, "and she is sure to say what you won't like."

"I can't help that," I muttered, utterly reckless in my disgusted misery. "My brain will burst if I don't speak to-night."

With a shrug he turned away, but his face was very pale, as he said :

"At any rate, get rid of Ella Maclise. Mother is generally careful before her, but you've heard enough already to be aware that she is not quite mistress of herself just now."

Acting on this suggestion I crossed to where the girl stood at some little distance off. Her tired eyes were dim with tears, and her whole aspect was one of grave anxiety.

"Good-night," I murmured, holding out

my hand to her—" good-night. This has
been a miserable evening for you, as well as
for me. But rest in peace; I promise you
that you shall never suffer such shame
again."

With a start she looked into my resolute
eyes.

" Be careful," she whispered. " Oh, Mr.
Perditus, I never saw her like this before;
perhaps she is ill."

" Perhaps she is," I replied.

Leading her to the door I pressed her
hand in mine and stood watching until she
had disappeared round the bend of the
winding staircase.

With a sigh I returned to the room to
find my mother angrily desiring Lucien to
re-fill her large glass of spirits and water.
My brother hesitated, and taking the glass
from his hand I put it down, and planting
myself immediately in front of our mother,
looked sternly down into the excited glittering eyes.

" Mother," I said very quietly, " you are

overdone and need rest, but before you go
there are a few words that I must say to
you."

Defiantly and sullenly she looked up at
me, but she did not speak.

" In the first place," I said, attacking the
smallest grievance first, " you must never
wear that necklace again ; you disgrace me
when you appear in such a miserable sham
as that."

Lucien had commenced to pace the room
nervously when he saw that I was prepared
to open the battle, but these words of mine
were evidently unexpected, and he stopped
abruptly.

" Sham ! " he exclaimed involuntarily,
with twitching white lips.

" A miserable sham ! " my mother repeated, the defiance in her eyes melting
into an expression of decided fear. " A
sham !   What do you mean, Friend, by
that ? "

" I mean," I said bitterly, " that with
your theatrical experience both you and

Lucien should have known the difference between these glaring imitations and the real thing. However, I shall not make a fuss about that; you have been imposed upon, and I shall suffer for it; I am willing to replace the necklace myself, if you will agree to certain conditions that I will impose upon you."

Still she did not speak, but she leant forward in her chair, clutching the arms with distended fingers, and gazing up at me with eyes of covetous eagerness.

"Mother," I continued, "these are my conditions. "You must promise me faithfully that you will never again subject me to such an exhibition as I have witnessed to-night. In fact, you must give up singing, except in the privacy of your own room, and you must also drop the acquaintance of Signor Maroni."

I had intended, when I began, to extract a promise from her also on the subject of her free use of cosmetics; but somehow, when I came to the point, I could not bring myself to mention it again. As it was I could see that I mortified her cruelly; her hard eyes actually grew moist; through the wash on her face I could see the red blood rush into her cheeks, and almost remorsefully I turned away while she recovered her composure.

I heard her give one or two short, gasping sobs, and then, with a smothered oath, she sprang to her feet, and, seizing my arm, turned me violently towards her.

"Listen to me," she cried, her eyes ablaze with fury. "I won't accept your insulting conditions; keep your diamonds, don't want them. I will wear what I like, I will do what I like, and I will receive whom I like in my own home."

I closed my hand over the fingers that clutched me so fiercely, and held her so at arm's length.

"In your own home you may do what you choose," I said, "but not in mine."

She started, and an uneasy doubt

quenched some of the wild beast rage which burnt in her eyes.

"Understand this," I said, "I will not share a home with any one who disgraces it."

"What will you do then," she asked, with a vain attempt to bluster, "turn out of it?"

"No," I said firmly, "I shall insist upon your leaving it. I shall provide for you, of course, elsewhere, but it was not in my compact to live with any one who makes me miserable. Now, choose at once. Do as I ask, or leave my house to-morrow."

Utterly subdued, the mortified woman released her hand from my grasp, and sinking into her chair again covered her face with her shaking fingers.

Going to her, Lucien knelt down in front of her and said in low, faltering tones:

"Mother, agree to Friend's conditions, they are not hard ones; your style is too strong for private rooms, and Maroni is a horrid cad. Agree to Friend's conditions, for my sake, mother."

Then, with a cry that really pierced me to the heart, the unhappy woman flung her arms round Lucien's neck and clung sobbing to him. I knew perfectly well her tears were not natural ones, but were rather the result of the fierce excitement to which she had lent herself, but nevertheless I was assailed with a painful feeling of compunction as she moaned and cried over the son for whom she had real affection.

"Oh, Lucien," she sobbed, "you know I will do anything for you, anything, anything; from the beginning it has all been for you."

"Hush, mother, hush," he said tremulously, "you are excited, you don't know what you say."

"Yes, I do," she continued, pushing him from her with a quick change from tenderness to fierceness. "I may be a little 'excited,' as you call it, but for all that I am cool enough to tell you that you have acted like a fool to-night, and that if you want me to put up with insults for your sake, you ought at least to do the best you can for yourself."

This burst of anger on her part was evidently as great a surprise to Lucien as to me; rising to his feet, he shrugged his shoulders in utter bewilderment.

" I have not the remotest idea what you mean," he said. "We are all getting muddled, I think, so for goodness sake let us go to bed."

" Not until you hear what I have to say," our mother replied obstinately. " Lucien, you are a fool to neglect Ella Maclise as you did to-night. Now that her fortune is almost within your grasp, after all these years of waiting, you are surely not going to be such an idiot as to let it slip through your fingers."

With a smothered cry, Lucien ran to her and bent over her.

" For mercy's sake, mother," he murmured in her ear, but not so low but that

in my startled wonder I could hear every
word; "for heaven's sake be silent. Go
to bed. Remember, Friend knows nothing
of this."

"Then," said my mother, rising with
a heavy maudlin laugh, "it's quite time
Friend did understand. I told him I would
explain a little more about Ella Maclise on
another occasion—well, this is a very fitting
opportunity, I think. I want him to know
me thoroughly to-night; I am no humbug."

My heart sank; whenever my mother
asserted this claim to sincerity, something
intensely repugnant was sure to follow.

"Friend," she continued, with a savage
sneer, which showed me plainly that, though
for Lucien's sake she had tacitly agreed to
my conditions, she hated me bitterly for
the slight I had put upon her; "Friend, it
has been a pleasure to you to act the part of
benefactor towards Ella Maclise, has it not?"

I made a gesture of assent, and she continued at once—

"Well, then, it won't be very agreeable

news to you to learn that we haven't been quite so disinterestedly charitable as you fancied. When I first offered a home to Ella Maclise I knew what nobody else knew in the world—for the rascally little lawyer who broke faith with his employer and told me, died the next day—I knew what even the girl herself is ignorant of, that she was sole heiress of an old uncle who lives the life of a hermit in some Indian wilderness. Two days ago I heard that the time we had waited so patiently for is near at hand now—the old man is dying of an incurable disease—and this is the moment Lucien selects to neglect the girl who fancies herself bound by the strongest ties of gratitude to us."

With these parting words my mother made me an ironical courtesy, and then walked unsteadily out of the room, leaving me absolutely transfixed with astonishment.

But no sooner had she disappeared than, with beating heart and throbbing brain, I turned to Lucien.

"Lucien," I cried, "What does she mean. Is she mad?"

"Half mad, I should say, to judge by her words and actions," he replied nervously. "Friend, go to bed, and forget this miserable scene. I am sorry from my heart that you should have been a witness to our mother's degradation. Good-night."

He walked hastily towards the door, and I was obliged to use absolute force to detain him.

"Stay a minute, Lucien," I said eagerly; "tell me what my mother meant. Is it true that Ella Maclise is an heiress?"

His dark eyes shifted uneasily under mine.

"Why, Friend," he faltered, "you surely would not attach any importance to mother's words to-night. Cannot you see that she is not quite sober?"

I winced. I was as well aware of this humiliating fact as he was, but it seemed to me so terrible to openly express such a judgment on our own mother. Lucien perceived my distress, and continued glibly—

"Friend, don't let us talk any more to-night; it is impossible, under the circumstances, to avoid wounding each other. Now, good-night."

But still I shook my head.

" No," I cried resolutely. " I must know what you can tell me on this subject."

There was an angry gleam in his dark eyes, but his manner was cool, as with his usual shrug of the shoulders he seated himself and began caressing his small black moustache.

" I can't tell you much," he said.

" But you know what mother knows, and she seems to be very *au fait* in the matter."

"Friend," Lucien responded, looking lazily and sleepily up into my excited face. "Don't you know mother well enough by this time to be aware that, when she wants to hurt your feelings, she invariably makes a point of representing her own character in the worst possibly light? She owes you a grudge to-night. Well, her way of paying it is singular, but her method is always successful, you must admit that; every time she lowers herself in your estimation she knows that she inflicts the severest punishment on you that is in her power."

"Do not beat about the bush, Lucien," I continued impatiently. "Tell me what I want to know. Is it true that Ella Maclise is likely to inherit a large fortune ? "

"Well," my brother replied with a reflective frown, "since you ask me I should say the matter is extremely problematical. She has a rich old uncle somewhere in the wilds, a religious fanatic, but whether she will get his money or not is quite an open question. The chances are it has been wormed out of the old fellow by dervishes and other followers of occult sciences long ago. Really and truly my mother has very little hope that Ella will inherit anything, and for that reason she has never told her of the possibility. Now good night, Friend, you know as much as I do. Don't repeat what you have heard to Ella, you might disappoint her cruelly; good night, and forget this uncomfortable evening as soon as you can."

" By-the-bye," he continued, putting his head in again at the door, " you needn't look upon our party as a failure, half-a-dozen of the best people in the room told mother they should send her invitations for coming receptions; don't you make any mistake, Friend, one has to be very strong indeed to shock society. Amuse them, make them laugh, whether at the expense of your dignity or not, and you are welcome; but bore them, and be you the most virtuous creature in existence, they will turn their backs upon you."

But my brother's philosophy fell upon unheeding ears. At that moment there was no room in my mind but for one thought, and that one thought was that, after all, Lucien's love for sweet Ella Maclise had not been a true one.

He might say what he liked, he could not
deceive me. There had been no mistaking
the earnestness of his desire to suppress his
mother's revelations, and, though his story
was a plausible one, I could not doubt that
in her fevered excitement our mother had
imprudently shown me their real belief.

In that case surely the bonds with which
I had inexorably crushed my own over-
mastering love might be loosed. Under the
altered aspect of the case I could recognise
no duty towards my brother which would
justify me in sacrificing myself, and possibly Ella – ah! at the thought how my
heart bounded in my breast!—on the altar
of this worldly interested affection.

And so after all I retired to rest with a
fluttering heart and a thankful spirit. And
ere I slept I took from a little cabinet in
my room a faded flower which had once
nestled against her fair bosom.

Again and again I pressed the withered
petals to my lips.

"My darling! my darling!" I murmured.

And then tears of happiness forced themselves from my eyes and fell upon the flower, which I could almost fancy revived and blossomed once more, as within my breast my parched heart grew strong in hope.

CHAPTER VII.

FOR some weeks after the eventful twenty-eighth of October it seemed as though a great happiness, hitherto only dreamt of, were really within the range of possibilities for me.

Unobserved by her I watched Ella Maclise carefully, and the more I saw of her the stronger my conviction grew that while she felt for my brother a sisterly affection, for me she entertained far warmer sentiments. She was very retiring, and there was at all times in her bearing a true maidenly dignity; nevertheless the tell-tale blood would rush to her cheeks when she met me suddenly, and her sweet eyes would sparkle with pleasure, whereas for Lucien no such evidences of feeling would be apparent.

For a few weeks, oblivious of everything else, I revelled in this new delight. I said no word to her; I did not want to interrupt the sweet dreams of bliss with which I was encompassed; but I watched her, and each day my devouring love for her grew more and more fervent.

So happy was I, and so entirely engrossed by this passion, which, held at bay for so long, raged all the more fiercely for the constraint that I had laid upon it, that I did not allow my mind to dwell on perplexities, which, even in the midst of my supreme delight, I was conscious loomed vaguely but substantially in the distance.

" No," I would cry, repelling the misty shadow, " get thee hence! Leave me! I will not think of thee! This sweet time is the green oasis in the arid desert of my life. Let me enjoy it for a spell; give me breathing time."

And then, thrusting my doubts aside, I

would rejoin Ella, and, sitting by her side listening to her animated description of her day's labour of love, I would give myself up once more to the witchery of her girlish fascination.

My intercourse with my mother, also, at this period was far less painful than it had been. I fancied that I perceived in her a genuine regret for what had transpired on the evening of our never-to-be-forgotten house-warming. She did not refer to the subject, it is true, but her whole bearing was quietly apologetic, and, being only too thankful to recognise this, I, on my part, willingly accepted her silent overtures; and before a week had passed, with Frank Nesbit, who was a judge of such matters, to assist me in my choice, I purchased a set of diamonds for her, which I presented, and she received, without reference to what had gone before.

But in singular contradiction, as Christmas—the symbolical period of peace and good will—drew near, my spirits grew more and more uneasy, and the vague shadow, which had haunted me even in the midst of my happiness, each day grew more tangible.

I loved Ella Maclise, and in my heart of hearts I knew she loved me. My duty towards my brother no longer stood in my path; but was there not another and even more insuperable obstacle?

Could I offer to this pure, noble-minded girl the love of a man who, for all I knew to the contrary, might in the past have been utterly unworthy to mate with her?

Distracted with these doubts, day after day I wrestled with them, one instant congratulating myself that I had for ever overthrown the restless demon of self-distrust which tortured me so cruelly, only to be utterly crushed the next.

Charlie Hall it was who, quite unconsciously, added the last straw to the burden which already lay so heavily upon me.

Frank Nesbit had been employed as senior counsel by an eminent firm of bankers in the prosecution of a young man who had committed forgery to a very serious extent. Frank had worked zealously for his clients in bringing the crime home to the unfortunate youth, and had received much praise and kudos for the way in which he had conducted the business.

Meeting him at Charlie's house one evening late in December I congratulated him on his triumph, for I had read that day in the "Times" how the forger, who was to all appearance a most unmitigated scamp, had been sentenced to a period of well-deserved penal servitude; and that in consequence of his brilliant success in conducting the case, Mr. Frank Nesbit would in all probability be invested with the honours of Q.C. before the New Year.

"Well," replied Frank, who I now perceived was not in his usual state of high spirits, "I am glad, Friend, that you think me deserving of a word of praise. I don't suppose any one would credit you with a cruel disposition. Charlie has been taking the conceit out of me to any extent, confound him."

In surprise I looked across at my old
friend. His eyes were very grave, and full
of wistful pity.

"Friend is carried away by his admiration
of your great talent, Frank; but I believe if
he thought about the matter he would feel
as I do," he said sadly. "You know there
is no one living who wishes you well more
heartily than I do, or who would rejoice
more in your success."

"Oh, it's all very well to say that;"
grumbled the other.   •

"It's the truth," cried Charlie, getting up
and pacing the room, while his young wife
looked anxiously after him; "but I can't find
it in my heart to congratulate you on this,
Frank. I wish from my soul that you had
not been quite so clever. The face of
that poor lad in the dock yesterday will
haunt me for many a week. Ah, Frank,
as you heaped up evidence upon evidence
against him, I could almost have cursed
your fatal eloquence. He was but nineteen
—scarcely a man—and twenty years of

penal servitude! Great heavens! it is a lifetime."

With an exclamation of anger, Frank Nesbit brought his hand down heavily upon the table.

" Oh, that's all sentimental nonsense ! " he cried hotly ; " the fellow was as thorough a scoundrel as any I have ever heard of. Why his whole life does not present one redeeming feature. He was a thief at school, and he has robbed systematically every one he has come in contact with—even those he was bound to by the very strongest ties of gratitude. Such a hound is not fit to be at large preying upon society. This is a case indeed when, as I said yesterday, we show most pity when we show justice, for then we ' pity those we do not know.' "

With a sigh Charlie seated himself.

" Nevertheless, Frank, I do commiserate that unfortunate creature from my heart. Granted that he is as bad as you represent him, and I see no reason to doubt it, he is still a being that claims our utmost sympathy. He is a thief and a rogue, but what made him so? Now, Frank Nesbit, on your honour as a man, do you hold that miserable boy responsible for his rascalities? What chance had he from the beginning? Was not his father a drunkard, and his mother one that no honest man could think of without the most bitter shame? From his cradle he lived in an atmosphere of sordid moral degradation, and knowing this can we venture to be hard on him? His mind was poisoned in childhood, and the more I see of life the more firmly convinced am I that out of such early surroundings as these no honourable man or woman ever came."

With a smothered exclamation I arose.

"Why, Friend, old man, what's the matter; you are not ill, are you?" Charlie cried.

"No," I murmured, "not to any extent; but I feel head-achy and faint, and I should be better in bed. Good-bye, old fellow.

No, no, don't come with me. Really and truly I would rather be alone."

But though I contrived to speak indifferently there was one there who guessed my secret. That one was Charlie Hall's wife, and in her bright eyes big tears of sympathy gathered, as in parting she pressed my hand in hers.

But once out in the street, away from those kindly inquisitive eyes, the agony of my mind forced itself from me in short gasps and moans of concentrated misery. Every word that had fallen from Charlie's lips rang in my excited brain until the clangour became almost insupportable.

"His mother was one that no honest man could think of without shame!" And again, "From his cradle he lived in an atmosphere of moral degradation; his mind was poisoned in childhood; from such early surroundings as these no honourable man or woman ever came."

I ground my teeth in anguish; Charlie had but given form to my own doubts and fears.

For my mother I had no respect, absolutely none, and I could not shut my eyes to the fact that, though my brother Lucien appeared to be a very modified edition of herself, still he had to some extent inherited her qualities, and there was a large amount of selfish worldliness and craft in his composition. How could I hope then that I was entirely free from this sordid contamination? At present these evil qualities appeared to be quiescent in me, but this condition might be the result of the complete severance with the past which proceeded from my loss of memory; or again, from the good influence which Charles Hall had exercised over me during the first months of my recovery. Could I be sure then if the day ever came when my memory should be restored to me that shifty dishonest proclivities, such as I shuddered to recognise in my mother, might not revive in me?"

Terribly agitated I paced the silent streets.

"If I had but an adviser to whom I

could apply," I murmured. " I dare not ask Charlie, his own words stand between him and me; and who else do I know who would have any power to console or strengthen me at such a moment as this?"

And then, with a start, I thought of the old French physician, Dr. Marion. Once before, in a time of sore distress of mind, he had lifted the burden from my shoulders and saved me from myself.

" Yes, I will go to him," I muttered; "if anyone in the world can help me, he can."

It was well nigh morning when at last I ceased my weary walking and entered my home; but though I was tired out mentally and physically I allowed myself no time to rest. Taking a sheet of paper I wrote a few words to my mother, telling her that important business had called me suddenly to Paris, and that I should not be able to accompany my brother and Ella to a ball which Frank Nesbit was giving on New Year's Eve.

As I folded this note I heard the first

milk-cart rattle by. Glancing at my watch
I saw that it was six o'clock. For more
than six hours, then, I had paced the
streets, blindly, miserably, wrestling with
my conscience.

Changing my evening dress for a thick
winter suit, and supplying myself with
rugs and cigars, I stole out of my room
again and down the stairs. As I opened
the house door I saw the first faint streaks
of daylight in the sky.

"There is a rift of light in the darkness,"
I said, "pray God it may be an omen for
me ! "

And then I turned, and looking up at the
window of Ella's room, I wrung my hands
and murmured passionately—

"Heaven bless my dear ! Heaven bless
her and comfort me ! "

Half an hour later I was speeding towards
Folkestone, and late the same afternoon I
stood upon the French physician's doorstep,
applying for admittance.

Perhaps it was as well for me that he

should have been absent on that afternoon; all day long I had not broken my fast, and it is more than probable, in my condition of weakness and exhaustion, that the interview with him would have completely unhinged me; as it was I was fain to make the best of the bitter disappointment the delay occasioned me, and to go to my hotel and dine and rest.

Notwithstanding my excitement I slept soundly that night, but the clock was only striking nine when I again mounted the physician's steps, and this time was admitted to his presence.

At the first moment the courtly old gentleman did not recognise me, so much the removal of my beard had altered me, but I had scarcely spoken two words before with French impulsiveness he seized me by both hands.

"Ah, I know you now!" he cried in his clear ringing voice. "I am glad to see you, Mr. Perditus, I was afraid you had forgotten there was an old Frenchman who

felt a warm interest in you. I have heard
of your wonderful success many a time, and
then I have thought that your mind was
pleasantly occupied, and that perhaps it was
better you should forget the hour we passed
together more than three years ago."

My heart smote me for my neglect of
this man, to whom indirectly I certainly
owed all my worldly prosperity. He
noticed my embarrassment and proceeded
at once.

"Forgive my want of courtesy, sir, in
receiving a guest with a reproach, believe
me it is only the real interest I feel in you
that has betrayed me into such an error.
Now accept my sincere congratulations on
your prosperity."

He held out his hand once more and I
placed mine in it; but I imagine there
was no warmth in my grasp; at any rate
he seemed to feel there was something
wanting, for looking earnestly in my eyes
he studied my face attentively for a minute,
and then said, with the sweet almost tender

inflection in his voice that I remembered so well—

"Mon ami, there is surely something wrong. Is it sympathy you want from me, or advice, or what?"

His kindness touched me, and seeing I had a difficulty in replying he turned his head from me, and delicately motioning me towards a chair which stood in deep shadow, he took another himself, and then said gravely—

"Give your sorrow words, my son, you can trust me without reserve; a physician holds a confidence sacred as a priest."

There was no need for him to assure me of that. No one could look into those clear penetrating grey eyes and question the absolute integrity of this true gentleman; but I was obliged to wait for a minute or two before I could trust myself to speak.

In my life I have met with two men— this old physician and Charlie Hall—whose voices are so inexpressibly sympathetic that in times of trouble, while it comforts

even to hear them speak, the emotion it
stirs in the sore heart is almost painful in
its intensity.

"Don't hurry, my son," continued Dr.
Marion kindly, "there is no need for haste;
though," he continued gently, "I would
gladly know what it is that weighs on your
heart and crushes your brave spirit. I
have had a long experience of life, nearly
seventy years, and many a trouble that
to a younger man seems insurmountable, to
me appears but a stumbling block which
is placed in our paths that we may have less
to regret as we see our end drawing near."

With infinite patience he listened to my
long disjointed story; and it was a relief
to me to find that his shrewd intelligence
grasped the situation exactly as it stood
without my having to dilate to any extent
on my mother's painful peculiarities; a
task from which I shrank with an instinc-
tive repugnance, although I recognised the
imperative necessity for his understanding
these peculiarities before he could possibly

gauge the distressing doubts of myself which
filled my mind.

A long silence ensued when at last I
came to an end, and then looking me
fixedly in the face the old man said—

"What is it you want me to tell you, my
son?"

"What I ought to do!" I cried. "Oh,
sir, I love her! You can never guess how
well!"

A gentle almost pitying smile came into
the clear eyes.

"Ah, no," he murmured, "of course I
cannot, and yet it seems but a day since
I married my wife. Ah, yes, a day since I
married her, but how many weary years
since I lost her? Well, the good God be
thanked, we shall soon meet now. But
come, mon ami, continue, you love her so
well you say."

"So well that I would gladly die for her,"
I murmured; "she is absolutely pure and
good and noble! Dare I then ask her to
link her fate with mine—over whose past so

dark a shadow rests, and whose mother—oh, sir, you understand me, I know."

With the same brave, steady light in his eyes which had shone there three years ago, when he awakened me from the deadly lethargy of my intense egotism, the old Frenchman rose to his feet and placed his hand on my shoulder.

"Friend Perditus!" he cried, and his tones rang out sharply and incisively as the word of command on a battle-field, "Friend Perditus, examine your soul—look into your heart—and tell me on your honour as a man and a Christian, do you recognise any reason in yourself why you are unfit to share the life of this pure girl whom you love so well?"

"No," I answered, with quickly beating heart, "I am true to her in every thought; but I fear to do her injustice."

"Then, my son," he said, "be very careful lest you do her the cruel injustice you are meditating now."

"What do you mean?" I exclaimed.

" Why this," he answered, patting me gently on the shoulder; " you did not say that she returned your affection; but I can read thoughts—you know that you have her heart, do you not? Ah, well, perhaps that is scarcely a fair question. Let us take it for granted that she loves you as well as you love her——"

" But that is impossible," I cried.

" Why? Because women are incapable of loving as truly as men? My son, the world's history teaches us differently to that."

" No, no; not for that reason."

" For what other, then? Because in your estimation you are not so worthy as she is? But from time immemorial women have chosen through their hearts, not their heads; and, my son, I don't want to flatter you, but many a woman has broken her heart over a less worthy man than you are. Therefore I can fancy that this young girl may love you very fondly."

" And what then, what then?" I cried, in

a transport. "If that is so, is it not my duty to save her from herself?"

"Listen to me," he said, very gravely, "if you lose this girl you lose your chance of happiness, is it not so?"

I bowed my head with a sobbing gasp.

"Well then, I will look at the matter from her point of view—if *she* loses your love, she loses *her* chance of happiness. Now I ask you, have you any right—because doubts of yourself are in your mind—to bring certain misery upon one who has done you the greatest honour that a woman can do a man, that of, unasked, bestowing her heart on him?"

"Doctor, doctor!" I cried, "be careful what you say. Oh, for the love of Heaven, be careful what you say."

Cheerily he clapped me on the back.

"Go to her, good true heart!" he said, "go to her! No mean soul ever looked through such eyes as yours. Torture yourself no longer, Friend Perditus; be happy, my son, and make her happy—it lies in your power, I am very sure of that. Mon ami, if, in answer to my earnest prayers, God had granted me the life of my little daughter, who died twenty long years ago, I would have given her to you without a pang, for you have an honest eye, a warm heart, and a conscience. Doubt not yourself," he went on, his voice ringing out again, "for a greater man than you or I—your own marvellous countryman has declared—' Our doubts are traitors, and make us lose the good we oft might win by fearing to attempt.'"

"There, there, my son," he continued tenderly, "I know what you would say, but you must not linger. Go to her; she is waiting for you, and maybe grieving for you. Adieu, mon ami, adieu; when the time of your happiness arrives, bid me to your marriage feast, and I will come."

What words I used I know not, but I have a confused recollection that I caught his delicate hand in mine, and that I even

bent my knee before him in grateful re-
verence as I carried it to my lips.

But when I left his house my whole
being was so transfigured with happiness
that I had hard work to keep myself at all
within reasonable bounds. As it was I
was conscious of attracting a good deal of
attention, as I marched along with my
head thrown back and my face glowing
with joy. For once, however, I was perfectly indifferent to the opinions of others;
and even when at last I was brought to
some sense of the eccentricity of so openly
parading my satisfaction, by the discovery
that my footsteps were being dogged by a
ragged little gamin who was endeavouring
to reproduce my jaunty step and proud
carriage of the head, I was by no means
uncomfortably embarrassed; but was able,
with perfect equanimity, to reprove the
urchin, and by way of enforcing my pre-
cepts, to give him a substantial tip into the
bargain.

It was a bright sunny morning, and

looking into the gaily arranged shop windows I was reminded on every side that it was New Year's Eve.

" And this is the evening of Frank's ball," I thought. " I can't regret having come, God forbid, but I would give a great deal to be with my darling there to-night. How lovely she will look ! "

Here I stopped suddenly ; opposite me was a railway advertisement, from which I learnt it was possible to reach London in ten hours.

I pulled out my watch, it was five minutes past ten. If I was lucky I still might arrive in time to accompany Ella and Lucien to the ball, and even if they had started I could follow them.

As quick as thought I hailed a *voiture,* and desired the driver to hasten at the top of his speed to the railway station. Arrived there, I found I had exactly half an hour to wait, and that, wind and tide proving favourable at Boulogne, I was likely to reach London shortly after nine.

Carried away by excitement, I rushed out of the station again.

"Who is the best florist in Paris?" I demanded.

"Delondre," replied a man.

"Can you drive there and back in twenty minutes?"

"Easily."

"You are certain?"

"Oh, m'sieu may make his mind quite comfortable; the horse is good and the distance short."

"Then," I said, holding up a ten franc piece, "you shall have this if you bring me back in time to catch the train."

The man scrambled to his seat, and it was well for me that no accident occurred, for the reckless manner he drove through the streets would at any other moment have brought my heart into my mouth.

It was also well for me that I happened to be the solitary occupant of the carriage in which I travelled from Paris to Boulogne, for had there been anyone to witness my

proceedings, I am sure I should have run
a great risk of being handed over to the
authorities as an escaped lunatic, when,
bouquet in hand, I flung myself into the
compartment, and fell upon the cushioned
seat in a paroxysm of amusement at the
horror-stricken gesticulations of the French
railway officials, from whose detaining
hands I had broken to rush after the
quickly moving train.

CHAPTER VIII.

How I fretted and fumed with impatience
as the train dashed through the glittering
frost - bound country, and what a bitter
contempt I felt for the persons who actually˙
appeared to think the weary ten minutes
at Amiens an insufficient time in which
to refresh themselves. To me the very idea
of meat and drink was insupportable, and
it is quite certain if it had been in my
power to deprive these voracious travellers
of their luncheon I would willingly have
done so. For once in my life my hungry
heart was satisfied, and, like all other people
in a similar situation, the grosser needs of
the body were altogether forgotten.

Ah, what castles in the air I built! What

visions of delight floated before my enraptured senses, and what a glow of joy
swept over me as, on the last stage of my
journey, I murmured to myself—

"To-night I will speak! Ere the new year
breaks I will know my fate; my happy
fate! Yes, I cannot doubt it."

I took up the bouquet and once more
unfolded the multitudinous sheets of silver
paper in which it was enveloped to make
sure that it was still uninjured. The pure
white of the fragrant flowers seemed to me
typical of my darling, and my whole heart
gushed out over them as I pressed my lips
to their snowy petals.

"Whisper my secret to her," I murmured;
"in your sweet breath carry my message
of love!"

And then I covered them up again and
thought, with a sigh of satisfaction, of how
Frank Nesbit's rambling old house was the
very place of all others in which to find
some sheltered nook where, secure from
interruption, I might tell my love, and

listen to those words which even to imagine set my heart beating so quickly that I was fain to open the carriage window and let the keen wintry air blow in upon my face.

The boat was half an hour late in reaching Folkestone, but the train made gallant efforts to recover the lost time, and it still wanted a quarter of an hour of ten when I drove up to my home. A closed carriage was opposite the house, and at the open door stood the footman. The man touched his hat as he recognised me.

" They have not started yet then, Tom ? " I inquired hurriedly.

" No, sir, the carriage was ordered at a quarter to ten."

" Then you had better tell Fred to walk the horses about a bit, it's very cold and we shall not be ready for another quarter of an hour or twenty minutes."

" Very well, sir."

Quickly I ran up the steps and into the hall.

"Where's Jarvis?" I said, asking for the man who acted as valet to my brother and me.

"Just come down from Mr. Guadella's room, sir," replied the butler, who was much too dignified a person to show any surprise at my unexpected appearance and excited manner.

"Then tell him to get my things out, and have the shaving tackle ready, I will be with him in two minutes. Come, hurry, Martin; I am going with Mr. Guadella and Miss Maclise, and I don't want to keep them waiting."

All this time I had been tearing off the white paper which enfolded the bouquet, tossing it here and there about the hall with utter disregard to appearances.

"Let the maids sweep that up," I cried, springing up the stairs. "I suppose I shall find the ladies in the boudoir?"

"Yes, sir, you will."

Almost roughly, for my impatience got the better of me at last, I burst into the room.

" Friend ! "

" Friend ! You here ? "

But forgetful of all conventional duty or respect, I paid no attention to my mother or brother. As I entered I heard Ella's soft murmur of " Mr. Perditus ! Oh, how glad I am ! " And, rushing to her, and, clasping the small white-gloved hand in mine, I stood for a moment speechless before the shrine of my idolatry, devouring with my eyes the lovely face which flushed so quickly under my eager gaze, and the slim figure, in its sheeny, silken gown of ivory white, which was not more satiny in texture or delicately pure in hue than was the soft creamy skin of its adorable wearer.

I was recalled to a sense of the necessity for self-control by feeling the little hand begin to tremble in mine, and by seeing that the bosom of the modest gown began to heave as though the intensity of my admiration were almost painful.

" I have brought you some flowers," I murmured, "and in return I want you to sit down and wait a few minutes while I dress. Will you ? "

" Why, of course I will—gladly," she replied, her face lighted up with smiles. " Oh, how good of you to have brought me these lovely flowers ! Are they not beautiful ? See, Mrs. Guadella ! See, Lucien ! And the ivory holder, too ! Oh, Mr. Perditus, you are too generous, really ! I have never seen so lovely a bouquet."

" I am glad you like it," I said, unable to suppress in my tone the tenderness which filled my heart to overflowing. " In Paris I, too, thought it perfect in its way, but somehow here it does not look by any means so well."

" But why ? The flowers are as fresh as possible. You must have taken good care of them indeed; not a spray of the fern even is withered.

" No," I replied, smiling at the questioning, happy face, " the flowers are the same; but when you hold them in your hand their beauty seems to be extinguished, and they

seem almost unworthy of your accept-
ance."

The compliment was a very clumsy one;
but possibly on that account it was all the
more unmistakable, and so vivid a flush
overspread Ella's cheek, that, a little
ashamed of having caused her such embarrassment, I turned quickly from her,
and found my mother and brother regard-
ing us with very disapproving eyes.

" Forgive me, mother," I said penitently,
hastening to her, and taking her unrespon-
sive fingers in mine. "I was anxious to
get those flowers off my hands before any
harm came to them. Now I cannot wait to
tell you how it is that I return so much
sooner than I expected, for I don't want
to keep Miss Maclise and Lucien waiting
longer than I need."

"What do you mean, Friend?" demanded
my mother harshly.

" Why, I am going to the ball with
them, I hurried home on purpose," I
continued, glancing with loving pride at

the white-robed figure, with its snowy mass of flowers.

"But you have to dress, and the horses can't stand at the door for an hour."

"I shall not be more than a quarter of an hour," I said merrily. "Ten minutes would be sufficient under ordinary circumstances, but Miss Maclise and Lucien are really so very magnificent that I feel I must bestow a little more attention than usual on myself to come at all near their exalted standard. The horses won't hurt, for I told Fred to keep them on the move."

I had half opened the room door when my mother, hastening after me, clutched me tightly by the arm.

"I am sorry to interfere with your pleasures," she said slowly, "but I particularly want to speak to you to-night."

"But not at this moment, mother, surely," I cried. "Won't it do when we return?"

"I shall not be up when you return,"

she replied harshly. " I must ask you to spare me a few minutes now."

" But," I said, in great vexation, " it's already late. I really hope you will excuse me to-night, mother. To-morrow I will hold myself entirely at your disposal."

" To-morrow will be too late for what I have to say. Surely, my son, it is no such great hardship, after an absence, to bestow a quarter of an hour upon your mother."

" An absence of twenty-four hours only," I answered curtly, chafing with annoyance. " Come, mother, be reasonable; the others have waited some time already."

" They need wait no longer," she replied promptly.

" How ? "

" Let them go now, and you can follow in a cab; if you feel inclined, that is, after our chat," she added maliciously.

With an exclamation of anger I turned from her. I did not feel that I could defy her openly, although I was certain in my own mind that she was detaining me simply with the ill-natured desire of spoiling my enjoyment, and so wreaking upon me her ill-humour and chagrin at not having been included in the invitation to Frank Nesbit's ball.

Going to Ella I offered her my arm.

"You must not wait for me," I murmured; "my mother wishes to speak with me, and I cannot refuse to listen."

A look of blank disappointment came into the fair face, and the red lips began to tremble piteously.

"Oh, I am so sorry," she whispered. "I don't care to go myself, now."

My heart bounded with joy; I was even cruel enough to revel in her distress.

"But why?" I said, as we left the room together. "You did not expect me to accompany you."

"I know that," she faltered, "but when you said you would come, I was so glad, so glad, and now——"

She turned her face from me, but I noticed the heaving of her breast, and I knew that there were tears in her gentle eyes.

Stopping in a bend of the stairs, where we were free from observation, I bent over her.

"Ella," I whispered tenderly, for the first time addressing her by her Christian name.

She looked quickly up at me in startled happiness; aye, there was no doubt of it, tears glistened in her eyes, but her whole face was radiant with happiness.

"Ella, I shall follow you very soon. My mother shall not detain me long. Will you keep some dances for me?"

She gazed at me with an ineffable look of shy tenderness, but before she could reply we heard Lucien shut the door of the room we had left, and run down the stairs after us.

Without another word we proceeded to the carriage, but when I had assisted her into it, and arranged the rugs carefully round her, so as not to crush her delicate dress, she pressed my hand gently.

"How many dances do you want?" she murmured.

"Eight, I replied promptly. "I shall not be satisfied with one less."

Returning her timid pressure, I drew back to let Lucien get in. Oh, how I envied him the drive with her! But as the light of the lamp fell upon his face my envy gave place to anxiety, and I uttered an involuntary exclamation of dismay.

"Why, Lucien!" I cried, "you are ill, surely. My dear boy, come in again; you must have something; you look awfully bad."

"It's nothing," he answered curtly, almost thrusting me away, "go to mother, Friend, she is waiting for you. There is nothing wrong with me."

But though his words were re-assuring, the memory of his ghastly face haunted me until I reached the boudoir.

"I am sorry for him," I murmured; "I am afraid after all he is really fond of my darling; probably he has guessed my intentions to-night, and is upset in consequence.

Well, I am sorry for him, but since she loves me I cannot break two hearts on his account."

I found my mother seated by the side of the table with her head leaning on her hand.

"Well, mother," I commenced, making no effort to conceal the annoyance I felt, "what is this important matter you want to speak about ? I can give you ten minutes. I have ordered the cab in half an hour."

"It was a pity to do that, Friend," she said, with a sneering smile, "you may not be ready in half an hour."

"I shall be ready," I replied hotly, "if you will speak."

Paying no heed to my fretful impatience, she rose, and with an elaborate caution which aroused an indefinable sense of uneasiness in my mind, carefully closed the door, which I had left open when I entered.

"We do not want eavesdroppers," she

said with ominous calmness, and then she
walked to a side table and poured out for
herself a glass of her favourite beverage,
brandy and soda water.

I was surprised to see that although her
manner was otherwise collected her hand
trembled violently, and that it was with
great difficulty she poured the spirit from
the heavy cut-glass bottle into the tumbler.

I made no remark, but I no longer
doubted that my mother had something of
real importance to tell me, and also that
Lucien must have been aware of the subject on which she wished to speak.

For a minute or two my mother sat still
drinking her spirits and water and glancing
up at me from time to time with a calcu-
lating furtive look in her eyes; but in a
short time I saw a bolder, fiercer expression
come into her face, and then, finishing the
contents of her glass at a draught, she rose
and came to where I stood tapping the
marble fender with my foot and gnawing
the ends of my moustache with impotent

anger. She looked me in the face boldly
enough, but I fancied for all her assumption of effrontery there was a certain uneasy
sense of fear about her as she said :

" Well, Friend, and what do you intend
me to understand from your manner ? "

This was such a very unexpected com-
mencement on her part that in surprise I
repeated involuntarily—

" What do I intend you to understand ?
With reference to what ? "

" With reference to Ella Maclise."

I started, and I felt my face grow crimson
under her merciless gaze.

" I don't understand you," I stammered,
turning my head away.

" Then you are more of a fool than I
thought," she replied. " But come, you
need not think to put me off with such an
answer as that. What new thought have
you in your mind to-night in connection
with Ella Maclise ? "

Driven to bay I turned upon her and
cried excitedly—

" Since you ask you shall know; I have no desire to keep it secret. I love Ella Maclise, I have loved her for six months, but until to-day I never thought the time would come when I should declare that love. It has come now; in an hour I shall tell her what I am telling you now, and to-morrow, please God, I shall present to you my future wife."

Again the old sardonic smile appeared on her bloodless lips.

" You feel so certain of success then, my son ?"

I did not answer her, indeed I felt it necessary to rule myself with an iron hand lest in my excitement and heat I should give expression to the feeling of rage with which her mocking face inspired me at that moment. She did not wait for me, however, but continued at once—

" But how about Lucien, Friend ? Does it not strike you that he has a prior claim on Ella Maclise's affection ? You have cared for her for six months, you say; are you wilfully forgetting what I told you in the summer, that your brother has loved her since they were boy and girl sweethearts five years ago?"

"He never loved her!" I cried passionately. "He loves the fortune that she is to inherit; you yourself let me into that secret."

With a cry of anger she interrupted me.

"Take care, take care, Friend Perditus," she hissed, "don't tempt me, for your own sake don't tempt me!"

"Don't tempt you to what?" I cried in a frenzy of angry impatience.

"To tell you the truth," she replied hoarsely.

"The truth?" I repeated.

"Yes, the truth. Come, promise me that you will abandon this intention; give me your word of honour that you will not interfere with your brother."

In utter astonishment I gazed at her. Was it possible that she could be in earnest? But while I hesitated she spoke again, and this time the deadly malice of her tone left no doubt of her sincerity.

"Come, promise me, or take the consequences of your obstinacy."

My blood began to run cold in my veins, and a curious difficulty in breathing came upon me, but I did not hesitate.

"I will promise nothing," I said resolutely. "While I believed in the truth of my brother's affection for this sweet girl I was absolutely loyal to him, and so I would have continued to the end, even though my own heart had broken under the strain; but now I see clearer, and I know that in the eyes of God and man the sacrifice of myself is no longer necessary."

My mother placed her hands on my shoulders, and advancing her vindictive face close to mine she gazed into my eyes, while her hot breath fanned my cheek.

"In other words, my son," she said with a cruel laugh, "you, too, are anxious to secure a fortune with your wife. Bah! You needn't look so virtuously indignant.

You give yourself very superior airs, but to those who know you well they appear singularly out of place."

" Mother," I panted, trying in vain to free myself from the grasp which weighed so heavily upon my shoulders, " mother, you know as well as I do that your cruel insinuations are entirely undeserved by me."

" I know nothing of the sort," she cried, " you kept silence while you believed her to be poor and dependent; now that you know her to be rich, you will speak. But you shall not have her, I am determined on that. I will prevent it."

" It is not in your power to do that," I replied firmly, looking down into the ferocious eyes. " If Ella Maclise loves me, I will marry her."

" It is not in my power, you say ? " she hissed. " Now, Friend Perditus, for the last time I ask you, will you give the girl up, or will you take the consequences of defying me ? "

" I will not give her up," I replied

stoutly, "and I defy you to do your worst."

For a minute longer she held me by the shoulders, looking into my face with so malignant an expression in her evil eyes, that with a shudder I turned mine away from her.

Releasing me, with a short guttural laugh she walked to an escritoir and unlocking it touched a spring which brought to light a deep secret drawer. From this drawer she took a carefully-folded newspaper and one or two photographs, and then returning to her chair she seated herself, and putting the paper on the table placed her heavy elbow upon it.

Pointing to a seat opposite her, she said slowly and deliberately :

" You had better sit down, my son, I have rather a long story to tell you."

My heart sank, her manner was so menacing and cold-blooded, but, endeavouring to hide the agitation and fear I felt, I replied boldly enough—

"I prefer to stand, thank you. Please make your story as short as possible, for I am anxious to be gone."

Again she laughed, and my blood curdled in my veins.

"I congratulate you, my son," she said, "you play your part well. I can easily imagine a silly girl, ignorant of your antecedents, might be fascinated by your golden hair and honest, blue gray eyes. Bah! Nature is a bungler after all."

I felt my face grow white, and my knees begin to tremble. Throughout the day the elation of my spirits had upheld me; but since eight o'clock that morning I had not broken my fast except for a dry biscuit and a glass of ale on board the channel steamer, my system was in reality exhausted, and my mother's incomprehensible words produced in me a sickening sensation of faintness.

Observing my condition she continued callously—

"You had better sit down, Friend. I

warn you my disclosures will not be exactly pleasant to you. I can very easily understand what you are feeling just now. Well, you are a fool to drive me to extremities. Come, it's not too late even now. Do what I ask and our interview is at an end."

There was an eager look in the cruel eyes which deceived me.

"She is trying to frighten me into submission," I thought, drawing a deep breath of relief. "She would not have succeeded, but I am glad she has shown me her cards; it makes me better able to cope with her."

Going to the side table I helped myself to a small quantity of brandy, and after I had drank it I returned to my position on the hearth-rug.

Leaning back in her chair, my mother watched my proceedings without speaking; but I saw that the eager look of expectancy had died out of her eyes, and that the mocking smile was again on her lips.

"Well," she said tauntingly, "what do you say?"

"Nothing," I replied sternly, "I am waiting for you to speak."

"Very well, then, so be it."

Resting her elbows on her knees she folded her clasped hands under her heavy jaw, and then said, in tones of inconceivable malignity—

"Friend, are you insatiable? Cannot you give up to Lucien the chance of this wealth? Surely you might stand aside and leave him free to win this. Recollect you have already built your own fortune on Ella Maclise's money; it is his turn now."

In utter bewilderment I gazed at her.

"In God's name what do you mean?" I cried.

Rising she came to me.

"You know what I mean, Friend," she muttered; "surely you must remember some of the old days."

"You are torturing me," I moaned; "you know I recollect nothing."

"Well, then," she said, "you were doubly

a fool to defy me. However, whatever unhappiness I cause you, recollect you have
brought it upon yourself. I would have
spared—aye, I swear before heaven I would
have spared you—and I will even now, if
you will give in to me."

She actually raised her hands in supplication towards me, but blindly I pushed
her away.

"You have said too much," I panted,
"or too little. Tell me what you mean;
as there is a God above us you shall
not stir from where you stand until you
tell me what you mean."

Her eyes dropped, and I noticed that
beads of moisture sprang out upon her
brow, as she continued in hoarse thick
tones—

"Friend, I told you that Ella Maclise's
father died of a terrible shock; that shock
was the loss of his entire fortune."

"Well?"

"Through the loss of that fortune Ella
Maclise became dependent upon me."

"I know that."

"But when I told you that she had claims upon me, and that in my own poverty I took this extra charge upon me, did you suspect nothing?"

"Suspect!" I cried.

"Did you not suspect," she went on, lowering her voice, "that I must have had stronger reasons than I explained to you for such an act?"

"I suspected nothing then," I replied in hopeless bewilderment, "but now I know that you had an interested reason for befriending this helpless, unsuspicious girl."

"Aye, unsuspicious you may well call her," she cried, her eyes flashing with anger. "Unsuspicious indeed! since she respects and possibly loves the man who robbed and indirectly killed her own father!"

The room reeled round, and a thousand flecks of light seemed to dance before my eyes, dazing and blinding me, as with a shriek I staggered backwards, and falling against the mantelpiece clutched with outspread fingers the heavy velvet draperies which hung at the sides.

"Robbed—robbed! did you say?" I panted. "Oh, if you are a woman, and not a devil, speak. Tell me it is not true. Oh, take everything I have; but, for the love of God, tell me it is not true."

She covered her eyes with her hand, and seeing this sign of softening in her, I flung myself on my knees at her feet.

" I will forgive you," I moaned; " I will forgive you freely for the agony you have caused me. Lucien shall share with me to the last farthing, only tell me that it is not true."

For a moment she seemed to hesitate, but then she continued coldly—

"You have only yourself to blame, my son. I would have spared you if I could— now you must hear me to the end."

Her quietness was even more terrifying to me than her violence had been, and my tongue clave to the roof of my mouth as, supporting myself by the arm of her chair, still on my knees, I swayed backwards and forwards in front of her.

Keeping her eyes averted, my mother went on with an effort—

" When you arrived in England, had you not upon your person a large number of valuable diamonds ? "

I nodded ; my trembling lips refused to form a word.

" How did those stones get into your possession, Friend ? "

" I do not know," I moaned.

" But I can tell you—unhappily I can tell you. You were a clerk in a private bank. One day—more than five years ago —Mr. Maclise placed in this bank, in your charge, forty thousand pounds worth of diamonds, and received your receipt for them. Three hours afterwards the manager of the bank found that the diamonds were missing, and that you had left the office evidently in a condition of the wildest excitement. From that moment till the

evening Lucien met you nine months ago
you were as much lost to us as if you had
been dead and buried. What I told you of
my debt to Mr. Maclise was not true. He
was a stranger to me, but in her destitute
condition his daughter did not hesitate to
accept the protection I offered. No, my
son, the real claim Ella Maclise had upon
my charity was this—my eldest son had
orphaned and beggared her."

With a scream I fell upon the floor at her
feet, writhing and moaning and praying aloud
for annihilation—for madness—for anything
that would deaden the horrible pain at my
heart and the agony of shame I suffered.

Presently I felt a trembling hand upon me,
and then I heard my mother falter out—

" You have driven me to this, Friend. I
could not let you marry this girl, knowing
what I knew; and besides, your brother
loves her—your brother who has suffered,
as I have suffered, shame and obloquy on
your account."

For a few moments longer I lay there

utterly crushed; and then, with a sense of remorseful horror of myself that no words can convey, I dragged myself to my feet again, and stumbled towards the table at which my mother sat. She had unfolded the paper by this time, and the first words my distracted eyes fell upon were these—

"Great diamond robbery at a bank. Disappearance of the suspected man."

"The account of your crime is here," my mother said; "all these years I have kept the miserable record by me. Will you read it?"

Mechanically I took the paper from her, but I could not decipher a single word—a thick mist rose between my eyes and the print.

"I cannot see," I moaned.

And then in low distinct tones my mother began to read aloud.

CHAPTER IX

"THE whole city of Calcutta has been thrown into a state of great excitement by a robbery of almost unparalleled effrontery, which has already led to a most tragic and pitiable result. Mr. Edward Maclise, who was for some years in business in Bombay as a merchant, last week expended a sum of forty thousand pounds in diamonds. Mr. Maclise was an eccentric man, and no one can exactly understand the reason of this large purchase, for it has now been ascertained that beyond this forty thousand he did not possess a couple of hundred pounds in the world.

"It is supposed that he intended selling the stones again, and that he hoped to make

a handsome profit on the transaction; but, as
the sequel will show, there is now no chance
of this mystery ever being made clear. On
Friday morning, at ten o'clock, Mr. Maclise
was seen to enter the door of Manton's
private bank. What transpired within the
bank is not known with any amount of
certainty, for Mr. Maclise was shown · at
once into the manager's private room.
The manager himself had not arrived
at this hour, and, the head clerk being
absent on his yearly holiday, Mr. Maclise
was attended to by John Sherwood, the
clerk in charge——"

My mother broke off here.

"Your name is John Sherwood, Friend;
your father's name was George Sherwood."

I made no reply. I was still stunned and
only half conscious, but yet the horrible
words that were falling from her lips indelibly
imprinted themselves on my memory.

My mother resumed her reading—

"In less than half an hour, having transacted his business, Mr. Maclise left the

bank, and at about eleven John Sherwood was observed by the porter to come out of the office. The man says he noticed the time particularly, for it was not usual for Mr. Sherwood to leave before the luncheon hour, especially when, in the absence of the manager and chief clerk, he was the principal person in authority. The porter came to the conclusion, however, from the fact that Sherwood's face was deathly white and very agitated, that he must be ill, and walked quickly after him to ascertain if this was the fact. Upon this, to his great surprise, Sherwood began to run, and the porter, feeling that he could not quit his post, returned to the bank and thought no more of the circumstance until, three hours afterwards, he was questioned by the manager, who had arrived in the interim, as to whether he could give any explanation of the absence of Mr. Sherwood, who it appeared, according to a junior clerk who was working in the outer office, had gone out at eleven o'clock and had never returned.

"The porter told what he knew of the matter, and it seems that the manager's suspicions were at once aroused. On the previous evening he had suggested to Mr. Maclise the advisibility of depositing his jewels in safe keeping, if only for a few days, while he made his arrangements for leaving the city; and knowing that he himself would be late at the bank next morning he had told him that his business would be attended to by the clerk in charge, John Sherwood, in whose hands his deposit would be perfectly secure.

"The following morning, however, the manager had heard rumours in connection with this same clerk, John Sherwood, which had caused him considerable uneasiness, and decided him, at great personal inconvenience, to get to the bank as quickly as possible. But, after all, he arrived at his post too late.

"For eight years John Sherwood has worked in Manton's bank, beginning as a lad of eighteen at the foot of the ladder, and rising gradually by dint of steady perseverance and great business abilities to a position only inferior to the managing clerk. The fact of so young a man being left in authority will show the respect and confidence in which he was held."

My mother paused for an instant, and then I heard the sound of a vehicle stopping at our door.

"They have come back!" I cried, starting to my feet. "Oh, let me get away, let me hide myself, I dare not look upon her face."

Hastily walking to the window, my mother pulled the blind aside.

"It is the cab that you ordered," she said, "shall it wait?"

With a moan I sank into my chair again and covered my miserable face with my hands. I could not bear that she should see the tears of agony which burst from my eyes as I thought of what had gone from me in the last half hour—self respect, and with it the love of the woman I adored.

Leaving me for an instant my mother

ordered the dismissal of the cab, and then returning, once more she took up the fatal paper and pitilessly she proceeded.

" Oh, God ! " I cried, interrupting the ghastly story, " oh, God, how can I bear it ? "

But inexorably she went on, and wiping the clammy moisture from my brow I bent my wretched head again, and forced myself to listen.

" For eight years John Sherwood's conduct had been unimpeachable, but on the morning of Mr. Maclise's visit to the bank certain reports had reached the ears of the manager which, although not absolutely condemnatory of John Sherwood, were by no means to his credit. It appears that several nights lately he has been seen in a house of by no means good repute, in the company of a band of young men who are well known idlers and loungers about the city. It is supposed that in this house gambling to a most serious extent goes on; anyway, John Sherwood was observed to have a large sum of money in his possession on the day following his final visit to this place; but the money evidently did not last long, for on the morning preceding the robbery he drew out of the bank the whole of his savings, which amounted to two hundred pounds, and on the very day of the unhappy occurrence he is said to have observed to one of the junior clerks in the office that he was in low spirits in consequence of a loss of money, which loss had come about through his reckless and foolish conduct.

"Very much disturbed in his mind the manager repaired to the bank, and hearing of Mr. Maclise's visit and John Sherwood's absence went at once into his private room. Opening with his own key the fireproof safe in the wall he searched for the diamonds, but unsuccessfully. Cautiously he then questioned the junior clerks and the porter, for although his own suspicions were aroused he was anxious to give the unhappy John Sherwood the full benefit of any doubt; but the answers to his questions were not by any means satisfactory. From one of the junior clerks he learnt that Sherwood had left hurriedly within an hour of Mr. Maclise, after borrowing twenty pounds of him, while the porter's evidence was of a seriously discomposing nature.

" Terribly alarmed, Mr. Foley (the manager) drove to Mr. Maclise's hotel, and there his worst fears were verified. Mr. Maclise, who seemed almost stunned by his misfortune, showed him the receipt for the diamonds with John Sherwood's signature affixed, and after that no further doubt was possible of the unfortunate young man's criminality.

" Leaving the unlucky gentleman in the care of the landlady of the hotel, Mr. Foley at once proceeded to give information to the police, but although little more than three hours had elapsed since the commission of the crime, in that short time the thief had managed to escape. From inquiries instituted by the detective who was at once put upon the case, it was elicited that at half-past twelve a young man answering the description of John Sherwood was seen upon the landing stage from which the big ships start, asking eagerly the whereabouts of a passenger steamer that was advertised to leave the port that very morning; but, curiously enough, the ship had steamed an hour before the arrival upon the scene of the supposed John Sherwood.

"It appears on hearing this that the young man uttered a cry of dismay, and seemed in a state of complete bewilderment and distraction, in fact so discomposed was he that the people round were much interested in his evident distress, and were greatly relieved on his account when they saw him, some ten minutes afterwards, in deep conversation with the skipper of a small trading vessel, who was evidently telling him something which afforded him considerable comfort. After this the two men entered a small boat together and were lost sight of among the ships of all sizes which were lying at anchor in the river.

"Further inquiries, however, brought to light this fact. The small trading vessel, the skipper of which it is believed is under some heavy obligation to John Sherwood, left the port of Calcutta within half an hour of this occurrence, although the ship was not supposed to start until three hours later. There can be little doubt, therefore, that on board this vessel the escaped thief is, and it is confidently hoped that on the arrival of the ship at her destination he may be immediately apprehended.

" I regret to say, however, that Sherwood's being brought to justice will be but a very sorry satisfaction after all ; for the laws of this country, although severe on this class of offender, do not provide anything like an adequate punishment for a crime the immediate result of which has been so terrible. Returning from his unsuccessful search, Mr. Foley at once went to Mr. Maclise, but though he tried to soften the blow by holding out an almost certain hope of capturing the runaway, the shock was too much for his listener, who succumbed at once to an apoplectic seizure, from which he never rallied."

At last there was a pause in this horrible record of unatoned crime, and with despair at my heart I lifted my head and stretched out my hand involuntarily for the paper.

" Why distress yourself further, Friend ?" my mother muttered, " the rest is all a moralising sermon on the enormity of your offence and the evil results of gambling. However, if it will be any satisfaction to you, read for yourself."

She folded the paper so as to bring the heading under my eyes, but I had not perused a single paragraph before, with a sob, I threw it down again. Where was the use, as she said, of going over the shameful history again ? I could see at a glance that my mother had exaggerated nothing.

" There is only one other thing that I have to show you in connection with the matter, my son," she said, "and that is this woodcut, which was published in a local paper the following week."

She held up before my shrinking eyes a coarse woodcut of the head of a young man in boating costume, and under this was printed :

" Portrait of John Sherwood, the diamond robber, from a photograph."

It was very rudely executed, but although the face was younger than my own the likeness was an undeniable one, and I shivered as I thought how easily I might be identified by any one interested in the matter as the unpunished thief.

" This," continued my mother, putting into my hand a cabinet photograph, "is the original from which the woodcut was re-produced. The photographer made use of the negative without my permission, you may be sure. I suppose he thought so long as he simply re-produced your head and spared your brother and me, we should have no cause of complaint ; at any rate he risked incurring the anger of such utterly crushed creatures as we were after your flight."

The cabinet photograph represented a group of three people seated in a boat, with a background of tropical foliage. These three persons were unmistakably my mother, my brother Lucien, and my-self."

" Here is another," she said, " taken with Lucien," and here one of yourself alone, at an earlier age, with your handwriting on the back."

In utter wretchedness I stared at the bright, hopeful young face, with its frank steadfast eyes and small downy moustache; but the honest eyes mocked me, and in the corners of the firm mouth I fancied I could discern a covert sneer, as though the owner were about to say—

" Put no faith in appearances; a fair and goodly outside may enshrine a cruel, grace-less spirit."

Mechanically I turned it over, and on

the back I read, John Sherwood; taken
April 16th, 1874, at the age of twenty-
one. And, though I paid no heed to this
at the time, I remember now that strangely
enough this old handwriting bore a singular resemblance to that I had acquired on
my recovery under Charles Hall's patient
teaching.

With a groan I threw the card down,
and pushed from me the hateful record of
my crime.

"Burn them," I cried; "destroy this
miserable evidence of my guilt; it kills me
to look upon it."

But, with a quick gesture of alarm, my
mother gathered the papers together, and
rising hastily deposited them once more in
the secret drawer of her escritoir.

"I do not wish to destroy them," she
said calmly, as she re-locked it, and put the
key in her pocket. "You are obstinate,
my son, sometimes."

Utterly subdued, I offered no opposition.
I knew what she meant perfectly well.

Even my dazed brain was capable of grasping the fact that she was preserving these papers with the sole intention of frightening me into submission to all her future caprices; but so deadened were all my energies by the awful calamity that had fallen upon me, that I could not summon to my assistance sufficient resolution to take the papers forcibly from her, and with my own hand commit them to the flames which danced and flickered in the ample grate.

Scarcely able to draw my breath—for the incubus of my crime seemed to weigh upon me with nightmare-like heaviness— I sat staring at the firelight with my haggard, half-blinded eyes. For a few minutes a dreary silence reigned in the room, during which I struggled hard to collect my scattered, numbed senses, but presently my mother's harsh discordant laugh smote upon my ears.

" Don't look so forlorn, my son," she said, " you have not done so badly after all."

I turned to her, but her features were blurred and indistinct; I could see nothing plainly.

"Don't you understand me?" she said; "you have really been a very lucky fellow. If you had your deserts at this moment you would be in a very different situation; and that you have not met with your deserts arises simply from the fact that Mr. Maclise left no one behind him to keep the police up to the mark. His daughter, a penniless girl of fifteen in a French convent school, could do nothing in the matter, while his fanatical old brother took no interest in that or anything else. Had Mr. Maclise lived he would have kept the detectives to their work, and your apprehension would have been certain. As it was, the matter was carried out in a half-hearted way, and, in consequence, at this moment you are one of the richest and most respected men in London, my son."

"If you have one grain of pity in your

heart," I groaned, "for Heaven's sake don't mock at me now. I am on the verge of madness at this moment; don't push me over the brink."

Rising, I walked unsteadily to the mantelpiece, and, leaning upon it, supported my aching head on my hand.

" I cannot think," I moaned. " It is useless trying to make any arrangements to-night, my brain feels half dead; but to-morrow the act of reparation shall be made, and then, and then——"

" What then ? "

" Why, then, if God is merciless to me, and leaves me the burden of this miserable existence, I will take the matter into my own hands and end it. What does it signify ? My soul has gone to perdition already."

" Ah, you are over-tired, my son," she replied, with cool indifference; " go to bed and rest. But, before you go, tell me, what is this act of reparation that you speak of ? "

"The only atonement that lies in my power," I answered, with a groan. "To-morrow I will return to Ella Maclise double the amount of money I stole from her father."

Crossing to my side, again she laid her hand upon my arm, and looked searchingly into my burning eyes.

"Do you, then," she murmured, "wish Ella Maclise to know that you are the cruel thief who broke her father's heart and ruined her altogether."

"God forbid!" I shrieked, retreating from her.

"Then how do you propose to offer her this large sum of money?"

I pressed my fevered hand over my fore-head, and stared blankly at her.

"I don't know," I muttered, "I am hopelessly confused to-night; to-morrow I shall find a way."

"You will never find a way of asking a young girl to accept a present of eighty thousand pounds."

"I must, I must!" I cried. "It is her right, and she shall have it."

Steadily she gazed at me, and then, tightening her grasp on my arm, she said, with slow deliberation—

"There is but one way in which it can be done, and very likely you will not agree to that."

"I would agree to anything in this world," I cried, "to ease my conscience of a part of this insupportable burden."

Advancing her face close to mine, my mother hissed in my ear—

"If Ella Maclise marries your brother, it could be done."

With a moan I shrank away from her.

"Listen to me," she continued. "I do not wish to threaten you, or to increase your sufferings, but you must understand this plainly : I remain silent on the subject of your past only so long as you do not thwart me with regard to Ella Maclise. If you wish her to continue ignorant of the truth you must do as I desire."

"I am at your mercy," I groaned. "I cannot protect myself even if you torture me to the death."

With a flippant laugh, she replied—

"You put things unpleasantly, my son. I have no wish to kill the goose that lays the golden eggs for me, be sure of that. Instead of reproaching me, you ought rather to thank me for showing you the way to ease your conscience."

I made no reply and she continued—

"When Ella Maclise marries your brother you can settle on her in his name any sum of money you like ; and, as his wife, she cannot refuse to accept it."

"But she will never marry him," I cried. "She does not love him."

And then the agony of my soul found vent in words, and lifting my clasped hands above my head I moaned aloud—

"Oh, my God, what shall I do, what shall I do ? Her heart was in her eyes when she looked into mine. How can I give her up ? Oh, pity me, and kill me now !"

Paying no attention to this outburst of anguish my mother proceeded with merciless precision.

" I will not attempt to argue that matter with you, Friend ; if it is any comfort to you to think the girl has preferred you to your brother, continue to believe it ; it is a matter of perfect indifference to me, for I know enough of women to be certain of this ; whatever passing fancy she may have had to be the mistress of your house and the sharer of your large fortune, that fancy will soon vanish under the influence of your indifference and neglect."

" My neglect ? " I panted.

" Certainly," was the inexorable reply. "If she is not to know the whole truth concerning you, she must also remain in ignorance that your manner to her to-night had any especial significance. Come, it is not much I ask of you, it is simply to avoid her and to leave your brother free to plead his cause."

" It is not much," I moaned. " You tear

my heart out of my breast and then you
tell me I need not suffer!"

With a shrug of the shoulders she turned
away.

"I am not responsible for your pain,"
she said sneeringly. "Surely you cannot
be surprised that some punishment for your
crime should be awarded to you; it is but
Divine justice, my son; you must not kick
against Providence. Why, in what are you
better than that miserable young man for
whom your clever friend Frank Nesbit
obtained twenty years of penal servitude
the other day?"

"Take care," I gasped, "for Heaven's
sake take care, don't tempt me to forget
that you are a woman and my mother."

With another shrug she walked towards
the door.

"You are excited," she said calmly, "and
I am tired; therefore I will leave you.
Think over my suggestion with regard to
the settlement. I am certain you will
find it the only feasible manner of dis-

charging your monetary obligation in that quarter."

" By-the-bye," she continued, pausing with her fingers upon the handle of the door. "Since I believe we are agreed that Miss Maclise is to remain in her present ignorance as to the identity of her generous host and the miserable young thief we have been speaking of; it will be well that you retain your present name. Unfortunately John Sherwood is well known to her by repute."

With this parting shaft, without one word of pity or of natural regret for the wreck of my life, she left me, and when the door closed upon her I sank into my chair, and flinging my arms upon the table, buried my head in them, and lay there stricken dumb and motionless by the intensity of my despair.

Hour after hour passed away; the fire died out in the grate, and the icy cold of the winter night seemed to wrap me round and deaden my sense of suffering; but pre-

sently I started to my feet with a muffled
scream. Semi-conscious as I was, a sound
had struck upon my ears. It was the
carriage bringing home my brother and my
lost love.

Blindly I staggered across the room and
gained the landing.

"Oh, Heaven, give me strength," I
moaned. "I cannot, I dare not look upon
her sweet face. Grant me but strength to
hide myself."

With frenzied efforts I dragged myself
up the stairs, my knees trembling beneath
me. I heard their voices below me, and
then I made a desperate rush, and gaining
my room, double locked the door and fell in
a heap on the floor.

CHAPTER X.

THE cold, gray dawn was breaking when at last I arose. For four hours I had lain there, unconscious of the progress of time, unconscious of everything save of one overwhelming and terrible fact—the fact that henceforth my life would be one unavailing regret; and that even if my existence were prolonged to the extremest limit, that I could never hope to outlive the horror and loathing of myself with which I was at present filled.

My mind was still in a condition of hopeless confusion, but my brain was clear enough even then to grasp the miserable certainty that my mother had spoken truly when she said that my only chance of relieving my soul, even of the monetary burden that lay upon it, was the chance of Ella Maclise marrying my brother; for how could I go to the woman that I worshipped with my whole being, and say—

"It was I that killed your father; through me you were cast upon the world destitute and friendless; for all your troubles and trials I am responsible, and I alone. I am the thief John Sherwood, who, in your sweet mind represents all that is cruel and worthless. Now that through my theft 'I am rich, let me pay you back with interest the money that I stole."

Could I hope that in her righteous indignation she would not spurn me from her? Could I imagine that she would accept at my hands this money that was the price of her father's life?

I did not hesitate to tell her the truth because I feared punishment. In many ways it would have been a relief to my burdened conscience to feel that I was in some measure expiating my crime; but I knew that if I told her she would neither accept the restitution of the money which was her right, nor would she deliver me up to justice. Therefore, by disgracing myself in her eyes, I should not only make her miserable, but I should deprive myself even of the sorry consolation of thinking that I had been at least an honest steward, and that, so far as money went, her fortune was, perhaps, more considerable now than it would have been had it remained in her father's hands.

Of the agony it cost me to think of my darling as my brother's wife I will say nothing, for it is entirely beyond my power to depict the utter misery of that maddening reflection.

On rising stiffly from the floor, I looked at my watch. It was half-past seven o'clock, and already the busy hum of life was commencing in the streets. Hastily I changed my clothes and bathed my burning head, the icy water affording me a temporary relief from the throbbing, bewildering pain in my temples and eyes.

At eight, furtively and secretly, I left the house, and proceeded towards the nearest cab-stand. The snow was falling as I walked, the cold seemed to strike to my heart; and with a shiver I recognised that the strange benumbed condition of my brain extended to my limbs. I could scarcely put one foot in front of the other, and, slowly as I progressed, I panted and gasped as I have seen runners do after the most violent exertions.

With a beating heart I stopped, and leant against a shop window. What if I should die before accomplishing my purpose? At the thought desperately I pulled myself together. There was no fear of death in my mind. At that moment, could I have chosen between life and death, I believe that I should not have hesitated for a single instant, but the thought of dying without having accomplished my purpose was unendurable to me.

At this moment a man emerged from the shop against which I leaned.

"Are you ill, sir?" he inquired.

"I am faint and cold," I gasped.

"Perhaps a cup of coffee would revive you, sir."

I started as I recollected that it was more than twenty-four hours since I had eaten.

"I have not breakfasted," I murmured, "perhaps it is that."

"No doubt of it, sir," replied the man promptly, assisting me into the shop which I now perceived was a restaurant, "for those who are unaccustomed to it, it is dangerous to go out this cold weather without eating. Sit quietly there, sir, by the fire and I will bring you something at once."

I forced the food down my throat, and in a very few minutes it became apparent to me that my physical condition was much improved. My blood seemed to flow freely again, and I drew my breath without difficulty. I could not blind myself to the fact, however, that with returning strength the wretchedness of my situation became more clearly defined.

I could think coherently and consecutively now, and so bitter were the thoughts that crowded into my harrassed brain, that but for the fixed resolve with which I had started out I should have regretted that I had made any effort to escape the hand of death that appeared to be laid upon me.

In my mind's eye I could picture the scene that was being enacted at that moment in my house.

The breakfast table with its snowy cloth and glittering silver equipage, the bright fire, and the slender girlish figure standing by it. I could imagine the sweet anxious eyes, and the little pucker between the smooth brows; I could see the startled expectant glance each time the door opened, and the wistful disappointment which succeeded.

The tears rose to my eyes, but brushing them away almost fiercely, I muttered—

"Poor fool, you think that she will regret you; but are you sure of it? Perhaps after all she did not care for you, and if she did by this time your mother may have turned her heart against you."

Quickly I left the restaurant and pursued my way. Two hours later, having transacted my business, I threw myself on a sofa in the reading room of my club, and thought over what I had done.

Drawing a paper from my pocket I read it carefully through. It was my will, signed and attested, and drawn out in proper legal form by a young lawyer with whom I had a slight acquaintance.

In this will I bequeathed to Ella Maclise the whole of the money which I had invested in Government securities, amounting to eighty thousand pounds. Folding the paper I put it in an envelope, which I carefully sealed. Then, rising, I went to the table and wrote—

" DEAR CHARLIE,

"The enclosed is my will. Will you take care of it for me? Without your permission I have appointed you and Frank Nesbit my executors. I am sorry that I was prevented coming to Frank's last night, but I was dead beat. Don't be surprised if you don't see me for a few days, business is rather pressing just now.

" Ever affectionately and gratefully yours,

"FRIEND PERDITUS."

I dispatched this letter to the post, and then listlessly I sat myself down in front of the fire. To a certain extent my mind was relieved, for I now felt that in the case of my death, which I could not help thinking would be the happiest circumstance for us all, Ella Maclise would have the means of enjoying every pleasure that money could procure for her.

It being New Year's Day, the club was empty, and throughout the weary after-noon, thoroughly exhausted mentally and physically, I sat there blinking at the bright fire-light and dozing in my chair.

But when the waiter came to inquire whether I would dine, I was recalled to the exigencies of my position. I could not absent myself from my own dinner table on the first night of the New Year without appearing very singular, and besides, what should I gain by putting off the dreaded meeting with Ella? Sooner or later I must face her, and the longer it was delayed the more difficult it would become; for I knew that my burden of guilt could not grow lighter as time progressed; and with the terrible thought in my mind that no mitigation of my present suffering was possible even in the far, far future, I went out into the darkness, and pursued my way homewards.

My mother and Ella were already in the drawing-room, and as I entered it I could not resist one quick, furtive look in the direction of the girl over whom my desolate heart yearned. At once I repented the weakness of having granted my love even this slight indulgence, for I saw that my dear was very pale and sad—that her delicate eyelids were swollen with weeping, and that there was a wistful look of reproach on her gentle face which brought a hard lump into my throat that, at the outset, threatened to unman me altogether.

But I could not doubt the meaning or the threat which my mother's fierce glance expressed. "Act in opposition to my wishes and I will tell her all the truth," I read there as plainly as though the sentence had been blazoned upon the wall in flaming characters of fire, and with those cruel eyes upon me I dared not trust myself to clasp Ella's hand in mine. Therefore, with a slight cold bow, and a muttered "good evening," I passed her by; and, walking to the other end of the room, ignored her involuntary start of astonishment at my singular want of courtesy, and with a sickening pain at my heart affected to show an interest in a heap of New Year's cards which were lying upon an occasional table.

One after another I lifted the pretty trifles, but my weary eyes distinguished nothing that was upon the cards. On my retina —to the exclusion of everything else—that startled, pale, appealing face was mirrored.

"Friend," said my mother, advancing to my side with her usual repulsive, mocking laugh, "you must make your peace with Ella, if you can. After your gallantry in presenting her with that bouquet, she won't accept my explanation of your non-appearance last night. So you see, my son, young men should be careful lest they mislead ladies with their floral offerings. I tell Ella that once settled in a comfortable chair, in front of a good fire, with a cigar between your teeth and a glass of grog in your hand, that you did not feel inclined to turn out into the cold again, even for the pleasure of a dance with her; but with the recollection of that bouquet, and your extremely chivalrous manner, in her mind, she actually doubts my words."

The suffocating lump in my throat grew

bigger and bigger, but I clenched my fists hard, and contrived to restrain myself, even when I heard my darling falter out—

"I could scarcely believe indeed that there was no other reason for your staying away, Mr. Perditus, when you had promised to come. I feared that you were ill."

With averted eyes I feebly stammered out—

"I was not ill, Miss Maclise. My mother was right in the main. I was tired, and I felt, that even if I did come, I should be a very indifferent partner."

"Well done, my son," hissed my mother in my ear; "see, her pride is aroused at once. It is astonishing how these gentle creatures can flare up if their *amour propre* is touched. That curling lip and flashing eye is worthy of a queen."

"Lucien," she continued, in low meaning tones to my brother, who came into the room at that moment, "Make yourself very agreeable to Ella to-night; she wants a little smoothing down, and Friend and I are both out of her good books."

Where is the need to pain myself by telling at length what followed this unspeakably wretched evening? For weeks I could see that Ella Maclise refused to believe in my fickleness; but, as time went forward, and I still either avoided her altogether or treated her with the scantiest courtesy possible in my position of host, I perceived that she began to recognise that my feelings had changed towards her, even if she had not made a mistake as to my meaning in the first instance.

But though she treated me at times with a degree of haughtiness which inexpressibly added to my unhappiness, there were other moments when she would fix her eyes upon me with so wistful and eager a question in them as to whether it could be indeed true that I had altered so utterly, that, tortured beyond my powers of endurance, I would quit the room hastily, nor would I return to my home until I knew that she had retired for the night.

Throughout this melancholy period the conduct of my brother Lucien was beyond reproach. With a sore heart I was bound to admit to myself how striking the contrast must appear between his unobtrusive but ever-ready chivalrous attention and my surly ungraciousness. And I noticed, too, that, though at first Ella did not respond to his advances, as the days went on and still my neglect of her continued, she began to find his forbearing, delicate kindness a great consolation under the mortification of my studied indifference.

In his behaviour to me, also, Lucien appeared to very great advantage. By tacit consent we avoided any allusion to the terrible circumstances of which my mother had acquainted me, but there was no mistaking the sympathy of his hearty grasp of my hand when we met in the morning, nor the deferential respect with which he habitually treated me.

Often this show of deference pained me terribly. It seemed so hollow a mockery, knowing what we both knew; but at these moments I would chide myself harshly for my ingratitude ; my brother's kindness might be mistaken, but I was bound to admit that it sat very gracefully upon him.

All day long I was absent from my home, for, in the vain endeavour to deaden my heart-ache, I threw myself heart and soul into the business of the firm of which I was practically the moving spirit. It did not appear to me at the time that the bustle and excitement of the vast enterprises on which we embarked procured me any mitigation of my sufferings, but I know now that they did to a considerable extent. To a man so bitterly humbled as I was in my inner consciousness, there was a satisfaction in the praises I received on every side. Scarcely a day passed on which I did not hear my young partners congratulated on their connection with me ; and it was soothing to me also to notice that, from the porter at the office door to the head clerk—a very respectable gentleman indeed with a heavy salary—there was not a face that did not grow brighter when I appeared.

I knew how different it would have been could they have guessed the shameful truth, and sometimes I would picture to myself the horror and amazement that would come into their kindly faces should the fatal secret ever ooze out ; but nevertheless their confidence was a comfort to me, and I verily believe at this time stood between me and madness.

Of Charlie Hall I saw little or nothing. Out of consideration for me, he seldom came to our house, for my mother disliked him, and made a point of exhibiting herself in the very worst possible light whenever he was present; and with the terrible knowledge in my mind of my own guilt and unworthiness, I dared not subject myself to his kindly inquiries. I could not tell him the truth ; my whole nature revolted against it. I felt that to read in his eyes

the disgust that such a revelation must
bring forth would kill me on the spot; and
though I longed for death as the only means
of emancipation from my present miseries,
I had not the fortitude to incur voluntarily
such a fate as that. His sympathy would
have been an immense boon to me, but
from his contemptuous pity I shrank.

Many evenings therefore I was obliged
to spend at my home, and mournfully I
would sit apart watching my brother and
Ella as they played and sang together;
while my mother, seated by my side, would
whisper in my ear how evident it was that
Lucien was making progress with the girl,
and what a pity it was that he had not more
confidence in himself; for that it would be
well for them to marry quickly, for Lucien's
mind being unsettled, he was, in consequence, becoming reckless with regard to
money matters.

And then, lowering her voice further, she
would invariably end with a request for a
cheque. Lucien could not make his very

liberal allowance sufficient, and according to her own accounts my mother had been severely taxed in order that he might meet his engagements.

At first I made a faint protest against this system of extortion, but my mother's wrath was so fiery that I never repeated my expostulations, but uncomplainingly handed over cheques for hundred after hundred.

After all, what did it matter? It was better to do that than to endure her sneering remarks—that if Lucien *were* inclined to gamble and bet I surely could not blame him; at any rate, *he* had been scrupulously *honest* in all his dealings, and no one could be surprised at his taking to wild courses in his present condition of uncertainty. Let him be but married, he would settle down at once, she was sure of that.

Once I expressed my doubts of this, and then my mother replied so meaningly that I shivered as though a blast of cold air had blown over me.

" I am surprised to hear you say that, my

son. I suppose you think it impossible for a man to perceive the error of *slight* derelictions from the paths of duty. Naturally you would argue in favour of the reformed criminal's becoming a very decent member of society."

But as the spring advanced, and there appeared to be no more definite understanding between Lucien and Ella, my mother began to fret and fume with impatience.

For several evenings she harped continually on this theme, finding a malicious pleasure in the misery she perceived the subject afforded me. I wondered she did not express her opinion of his tardiness as a lover to Lucien, but I must admit that I was very much astonished when at last she boldly attacked the subject in my presence.

Ella Maclise was spending the afternoon at the Nesbits, and I knew that for more than half an hour my mother and Lucien had been closeted together in her boudoir. It was therefore a great surprise to me that she should have waited for my entry before she broached such a delicate and private matter.

Lucien appeared to agree with me in this, for I noticed when my mother bluntly attacked him, that he left the chair in which he was sitting, and, with a very white face, retreated to one that stood in deep shadow cast by the heavy crimson velvet curtains.

"Come, Lucien," my mother persisted, "it's no good your trying to get out of answering me. I am tired of this sort of thing. The whole house is unsettled, and it's not fair to the girl. It's quite time you came to a conclusion one way or the other."

"I have come to a conclusion with regard to my own feelings, you know that, mother, well enough," he faltered, shading his eyes with his hand.

"Well, then what are you hesitating for, in the name of goodness?"

I rose, my brother's evident embarrassment under this cruel questioning pained me, but before I could take a step my mother continued—

" Now Friend, for mercy's sake don't you go slinking away as usual; I want you to hear what I have to say, and also your brother's answer."

" If you mean why don't I make Ella Maclise an offer of marriage, I will tell you, mother," Lucien stammered.

" That is what I mean of course."

" Well then," he said, speaking brokenly and with a great effort, " I have not told her of my love because I fear that she would refuse me."

" But why ? " exclaimed my mother angrily, " she used to be fond of you, when you were poor and by no means such a good match as you would be now."

" I know that," he faltered. " In the old days she did care for me, but that was before——"

" Before what ? "

Glancing deprecatingly at me, Lucien murmured—

" Before she knew, Friend."

Our mother broke into an exclamation of pettish contemptuous annoyance, but raising his hand and speaking very earnestly Lucien silenced her.

" Yes, mother, it is the truth ; before she knew Friend she loved me, I believe ; but in comparison with him what must I appear in her eyes ? Ah, you need not sneer at me. I am not blind. I know that when I stand by Friend's side no woman will look at me, even. Why, you have said so yourself you know ; many a time you have twittted me with being his inferior in every respect, how can you wonder therefore that Ella Maclise should prefer him ? "

My mother received this outburst far more quietly than I expected, and there was a momentary pause before she said musingly—

" You may be right, Lucien, but still Ella Maclise is not the sort of girl to throw her love away upon a man who does not want it."

"But," continued Lucien earnestly, "how do we know that she is certain he does not want it, mother? Friend's strange avoidance of her is inexplicable to her; and while she is doubtful as to his sentiments I dare not speak to her."

"What would you have me do, brother," I cried in despair. "I love her, surely you know that?"

"I feared it," he answered with drooping head.

"But he cannot marry her, Lucien!" exclaimed my mother eagerly.

My brother sat quite silent for a moment, and then, with his head averted, he murmured brokenly—

"And why should he not marry her?"

I stared at him in blank bewilderment, while my mother starting from her chair commenced pacing the room in unrestrained excitement.

"You must be mad, Lucien, to ask such a question;" she muttered, addressing him but fixing me steadily with her steely eyes.

" Do you think that Ella Maclise would consent to marry John Sherwood the runaway thief ? "

" Ah, for Heaven's sake," I groaned, but my brother interrupted me.

" No, mother," he faltered, turning his face still further from us, " she would not marry John Sherwood wittingly, but she does not identify Friend with that unhappy man, nor need she ever."

" How do you mean ? " cried my mother, stopping short in her restless pacing to and fro.

" Mother," my brother continued brokenly, " you and I alone know the truth of this miserable affair ; so long as we keep silence, Friend's secret is safe."

" Well ? "

" Friend has been very good and generous to us—— "

" Ah, I see," sneered my mother, " you are grateful to your brother, eh, my son ? and you propose to give up the girl you love as a little return for his hospitality."

"I should wish neither to betray my brother nor to marry a woman who believes him more worthy of her love," said Lucien bravely.

With an impatient shrug of her shoulders our mother replied:

"Don't deceive yourself, Lucien, into thinking you will be doing Friend any service by withdrawing from your suit, for I am quite determined to be no party in betraying Ella Maclise into such an unnatural marriage as that would be. Of course with regard to your own affair you must do as you like, and if you no longer care for the girl—"

"It is not that, mother, you know I care for her," my brother cried warmly. "At first I confess I was attracted by her money, but now, if I thought I could make her happy, I would marry her, even if she had not a penny in the wide world. I love her for herself now."

Ah me, how easily I could believe that! and as I gazed at my brother with his glowing eyes and flushed cheeks, how well I could imagine a young girl returning this love with equal warmth.

" And yet," continued our mother with inexorable calmness, " you would stand aside and let your brother win this peerless girl; your brother, who dares not claim the name he has tarnished; your brother, from whom, if she but knew the truth, she would shrink with utter loathing."

" Mother, mother," pleaded Lucien, " it might be that she would not marry him, indeed I do not think she could do so under the circumstances, but you do her an injustice; if Ella knew the truth, I am sure she would feel for Friend, as I do, an immense pity and sympathy."

" Friend," he went on, coming to where I sat and stretching out his trembling hand, " I have not spoken on this subject, I did not feel that I could; but, brother, whatever you did in the past, you are at least in the present a man that commands respect and affection. I am sorry from my heart that our mother's interest in my welfare should have urged her into betraying to you this ghastly secret; as she will acknowledge I begged her to spare you, for indeed I would not have caused you the agony that you suffer, even though I knew that my happiness with Ella were secured by it."

"I am very sorry for you, Friend," he continued softly. "Heaven only knows how strong the temptation must have been to which so good a man succumbed. I am sorry for you. I have not lived with you for nearly a year, I have not seen your glorious generosity, without loving you and grieving with you."

They were the first words of kindness that had fallen upon my ears for months—for, as I have said, between Charlie Hall and me a coolness had arisen—and, touched to the quick, I grasped my brother with one hand, and placing the other on his shoulder I bent my head down on it.

" Lucien," I murmured with a sob, for at his gentle words my tears began to flow, despite my utmost efforts to restrain them, " Lucien, you must be happy at least."

" Oh, that's all very well," our mother interrupted harshly, " but you hear what he says, that while Ella is uncertain about you she will not listen to him."

" Then her uncertainty shall last no longer," I said in stony despair.

I felt a quiver run through my brother's upright, graceful figure.

" What do you mean, Friend ? "

" I mean, that I am grateful to you, Lucien, for your loving, pitying words, but that I should not accept the sacrifice you offer me, even if my mother would allow it ; I could not marry Ella Maclise, though I knew she were willing to share my life ; my crime stands between us."

" But she knows nothing of this determination of yours," Lucien murmured sadly.

" She shall know it before another day

passes over our heads," I replied; "you at least shall be happy, if I can accomplish it."

He wrung my hand hard.

"Oh, Friend," he faltered, "how can I thank you? She loved me once; in time her affection may return."

"Please God it may." I groaned; pushing him gently from me, and notwithstanding the bitter pang at my heart, the prayer was a very sincere one.

For the first time I felt a respect for my younger brother; he had shown himself truly generous and unselfish; and recognising these nobler qualities in him, I tried to persuade myself that I should not suffer so severely in relinquishing Ella to him. My own outlook was a dreary one, indeed, but I thought that if by my means happiness could be secured to these two young people, surely in time some faint reflection of their content and peace might come to shine on me.

CHAPTER XI

AFTER giving my brother this assurance, I fell into a deep reverie, so deep indeed that I did not notice at the time when he and my mother quitted the room; but a recollection comes to me now of the careful closing of the door, and then of a burst of excited conversation which faded away into silence as they descended the stairs together.

My position was indeed a very difficult one; how would it be possible for me to speak to Ella Maclise on such a subject without arousing her maidenly pride and incurring her just displeasure? And yet I felt that it would be better for us all that the doubts in her mind should be removed.

My mother's wishes on this subject, however, did not influence me in the smallest degree. I had long ere this recognised the fact that between us there could never be the slightest sympathy, and therefore so long as I supplied her with unlimited means of enjoyment, I felt that my duty towards her was complete.

I hope I can truly say, that at the best of times I have little self-conceit in my composition, though possibly this very assertion is a manifestation to the contrary ; anyway, at that period of bitter shame and self-reproach, it was difficult to imagine that Ella Maclise's affection for me could be a very deep one.

On the night of the ball she certainly had given me some encouragement; and with the recollection in her mind of the open glance of affection and the hand pressure that she had bestowed upon me, it was possible she might consider herself pledged in some way to me, and not free to accept my brother's more welcome attentions, even though, under the influence of my studied neglect, her sentiments towards me had changed.

Be sure I did her no injustice in my mind; I never loved her more truly and entirely than I did while I sat considering how I might best plead my brother's cause with her. To associate fickleness or caprice with her steadfast nature was impossible; but we know that love begets love, and coldness coldness, therefore it would have been only natural and right that Lucien and I should change places in her estimation.

I could not doubt that a marriage with this sweet, high-minded girl would have an extremely beneficial effect upon Lucien's character, which I believed, notwithstanding the pernicious influence of his bringing up, although somewhat weak and easily led, to be in the main kindly, considerate, and gentlemanly. With all his better feelings worked upon, what might he not become in the future? I could easily imagine, as he said, that with a wife and a home of his own, and such a wife, he would have an incentive to work, and that his present reckless courses would become hateful to him.

For this reckless conduct, too, I could not find it in my heart to blame him. If he gambled and betted, so had I for three long years under the cloak of business, the only difference being that whereas I had been lucky he had been unfortunate. The same spirit had actuated us both, and I could not forget how severe a shock had been necessary to turn me from my eager, illegitimate pursuit of wealth.

Then, again, if he married Ella, I could settle the eighty thousand pounds on her; and, even supposing she inherited nothing from her uncle, which was more than possible, with the two thousand a year that I intended to allow Lucien their future would be secure. I felt confident, with these new responsibilities upon him, that my brother would come to me for advice, and therefore I should be able to watch over the well-being of this household in which all my future interests would centre.

These were the arguments that remorselessly I brought to bear upon the subject; but, though I recognised their justice, and the strong reasons for carrying my purpose into effect, my rebellious heart sank so low that I can well believe no unhappy wretch on his way to the scaffold ever shrank and trembled more in spirit than I did at the moment my unhappy reverie was interrupted by the entrance of the one whose presence was a mingled torture and joy to me.

On seeing that I was alone in the room, Ella Maclise, with a quick flush, retreated towards the door. Deliberately I placed myself in her way. In my desperation I was aware that if I missed this opportunity another might not present itself for days;

and how could I depend upon my wavering
courage not deserting me altogether ?

"Miss Maclise," I said, so coldly that
I started at the utter dreariness of my own
voice : "Miss Maclise, there is something
I wish to say to you. Can you listen to
me now ? "

She did not reply for an instant, but
with my lowered eyes—for I dared not look
her in the face—I saw her white fingers
close so convulsively upon a fan she held
in her hand that, crushed and torn, the
delicate feathers fluttered to the ground in
a snowy shower.

"I will listen to you, of course, Mr.
Perditus," she murmured at length, walking
from me and seating herself in a *prie dieu*
chair.

Her fair head drooped forward, and the
dejected listless attitude touched me to the
heart. It was the first time we had been
alone since the fatal New Year's Eve. Ah,
me ! what it cost me not to clasp her in
my arms, not to pillow that dear pale face

on my breast, while I whispered in her ear the words of love that threatened to force themselves from me!

Sternly battling with this tender emotion, I turned my eyes away from her, and said with assumed calmness—

"Miss Maclise, I wish to speak to you on the subject of my brother."

She gave a start, and then she began to tremble violently.

"About your brother?" she gasped.

Ignoring her agitation, I continued in the same tone—

"Yes, I am anxious on his account; he seems very unhappy and unsettled, and altogether to have lost confidence in himself."

She lifted her shaking hand to her face, so as to shield it from my observation, and then she murmured brokenly—

"And from what do you think this change in him arises?"

My brain grew dizzy under the terrible strain, and my heart beat so loudly I felt

that every throb must be audible to her;
but I was resolved to go through my task
even though I died in the effort. With
all my determination, however, I could not
keep a tremor out of my voice, as I replied
unsteadily—

" He is unhappy because he thinks you
no longer care for him."

I saw her shrink from me and put her
other hand up to her face. I waited for a
moment, but then, as she did not reply,
steeling myself, I continued—

" Miss Maclise, my brother has been very
faithful to you. For five years he tells me
he has loved you devotedly. I know you
have a right to resent my speaking to you
on the subject; but it grieves me to see
him so unhappy and so doubtful of himself.
May I not give him one word of comfort
and reassurance ? "

There was a long pause, and then, with a
piteous quaver in her voice, she faltered out—

" Do you, then, wish me—to—marry—
your brother ? "

"Yes," I said, abandoning my cold tone, and speaking with great earnestness and emphasis, " I do wish it. I am not a happy man; there are circumstances in my life which stand between me and happiness; but there is nothing in the world that would bring me so much comfort as your marriage with my brother. I am very lonely, with few interests and few affections. Will you not bring into my dreary existence a new interest ? Will you not give me a sister to love and protect ? You see," I faltered, " that after all I am pleading on my brother's behalf in a very selfish spirit. I only want you to understand that in making him happy you also confer a benefit on me. In the natural course of events, if you do not listen to Lucien, you will marry some one else, and, believe me, he would not grieve more truly for the wife he had lost than I should for the sister in whose home I hoped sometimes to find content and peace."

"Oh, my heart ! my heart ! " she wailed

out, as the tears came stealing through
her fingers, and dropped heavily upon her
dress.

The dull pain in my breast grew intensified, and, bending towards her, I murmured
brokenly—

"Forgive me! forgive me! I would not
grieve you; I would die sooner. If you
feel that you cannot love my brother,
heaven forbid that I should urge his suit
upon you. It is only that I would fain
have you near me that I speak. Come, my
sister, dry your tears. I will ask you for
no answer now; only think of what I have
said."

And then, in an instant losing control
over myself, I broke out passionately,

"Oh, God! my fate is too hard to bear!
Must I bring sorrow and suffering upon
every one?—even those whom I would give
my life to save from either!"

"Ah, don't say that," she moaned. "I
would not add to your unhappiness for the
world. You must not think seriously of a

woman's tears. Why," she continued, with
a pitiful attempt to speak lightly and cheerfully—" why, they are proverbially near the
surface. We do not cry always because we
are sorrowful; pride or happiness will bring
the tears to our eyes as quickly as grief."

Rising, still holding the handkerchief to
her face, she walked somewhat unsteadily
towards the door. When she reached it,
with her head turned from me, she murmured—

" I cannot give you an answer now, Mr.
Perditus, but tell your brother that I will
think over what you have said quietly and
seriously in my room this evening, and that
to-morrow if he asks me I will reply. Will
you also beg your mother to excuse me
from dinner, I—I am not very well—
and——"

In an hysterical paroxysm the tears broke
forth again, but before I could reach her
side she had torn the door open and fled
from me up the stairs.

In blank despair I was still standing

motionless when my mother entered the room with a noisy bustle. Slamming the door behind her she came close up to me.

" Well ? " she panted. " Well, what news ? "

With a deep sigh I roused myself.

" She will marry him, I think, mother," I said drearily. " If Lucien speaks, she will give him his answer to-morrow."

" Very well, then he *shall* speak," my mother responded triumphantly. " I mean to get this matter settled as quickly as possible. There has been enough shilly shallying already. If she accepts him, and I presume she will, they shall be married in three months ; so, my son, you must make your arrangements about these settlements, for failing this old Indian fellow—and upon my soul from what I hear I believe the old boy means to live a hundred years—the young couple won't be too well provided for."

With another strident laugh she left me, and then wearily I sank into a chair and taking up a book endeavoured to fix my attention upon it. But the attempt was entirely in vain. Paragraph after paragraph I read, but they were meaningless to me; my ears were full of the words Ella Maclise had spoken, and presently it appeared to me that in the book I held in my hand they were re-produced on every line and in every page.

"We do not cry always because we are sorrowful; pride or happiness will bring the tears to our eyes as quickly as grief."

CHAPTER XII.

I DID not see Ella Maclise the next morning at breakfast, but when I returned in the afternoon my brother met me in the hall with a very radiant face.

"Come into the library, Friend," he murmured, "I have something to say."

I knew what that something was, but I was scarcely prepared for the sight of Ella herself, and had hard work to preserve my calmness when Lucien, taking her by the hand, led her towards me.

"Friend," he faltered, "you had already strong claims on my gratitude, but now you have laid me under an obligation that I cannot attempt to pay, except in this way.

Ella has promised to be my wife, and my wife is your sister, Friend."

My eyes were very misty, but grasping a hand of each I managed to keep my voice steady as I said—

" God bless you both, my brother and sister ; I am happy in your happiness."

" Is that really so, Mr. Perditus ? " she murmured wistfully.

" Mr. Perditus no longer," I replied, ignoring her question, " for my sister I am Friend." •

And so Lucien and Ella became engaged, and although my heart was inexpressibly sore at the loss of my love, on the whole it was a consolation to me to reflect that in future I should have a brother's right to stand between her and ill fortune ; that I could in fact watch over her home and interests, and by my advice and influence help her husband to obtain a position in the world worthy of her respect.

A few more kindly words passed between us, and then I left my brother and his affianced wife and went to seek my mother.

On my way to the boudoir my eye was attracted to a foreign envelope which lay upon the stairs. Picking it up I perceived the Calcutta postmark upon it, and that it was addressed to my mother.

"It has fallen off the letter tray, I suppose," I muttered, and then turning it over in my hand, I noticed that it had already been opened.

"Ah," thought I to myself, "my mother spoke from late information, then, when she predicted a long life for old Mr. Maclise. Well, after all I am not sorry for it. Lucien will be quite sufficiently well off, and his position will be more dignified in the eyes of his wife than if he had married her as an heiress."

"Mother," I said, entering the room, "I found this letter upon the stairs; I suppose you dropped it."

Accustomed as I was to my mother's eccentricities of conduct, I must admit I was very much taken aback when, with a cry of rage, she sprang at me and twitched the letter out of my fingers.

"What do you mean by interfering with my correspondence," she cried, glaring at me. "How dare you touch my letters?"

"Another time I will leave them on the stairs for the servants to read," I replied coldly; "I fancied I was doing you a service by returning it to you, but as usual I was mistaken."

She made a strong effort to recover herself, and then she said, with almost an apologetic air—

"I am not myself this afternoon, Friend; I have a headache, and I have been much worried lately on Lucien's account. I find the reaction almost painful. Of course I am obliged to you for bringing me the letter. Can you guess what news it contains?"

"Why, yes," I answered wearily; "I understood from you yesterday that old Mr. Maclise was better, and likely to live for many years; but I had no idea that your news of him was so recent."

Although it was the beginning of June, the weather being chilly, we still found a fire pleasant in the afternoons. Hastily taking the letter out, my mother crumpled the thin envelope up in her hand and threw it into the flames; and then, looking me fixedly in the eyes, she said slowly—

" Friend, since I spoke to you yesterday, I have heard again from India, and very important news, too. This afternoon I received this letter, which informs me that Mr. Macliso died a month ago, and that Ella inherits the whole of his fortune, which however does not amount to as much as we expected, being fifty thousand pounds only."

" You heard this afternoon ? " I cried, in astonishment.

" This afternoon," repeated my mother firmly.

" What, before Lucien proposed to Ella ? "

" No, two hours later, fortunately ; otherwise she might have had some suspicions as to his motives."

" Two hours later," I repeated in great bewilderment, " how extraordinary ! Does she know it now ? "

" Does she know it ? " cried my mother indignantly; " of course she knows it. You don't suppose I should feel justified in concealing such news as that from her. Besides there was an enclosure in my envelope for her which I was bound to deliver at once, giving her formal information of her accession to wealth. I wish you had been there to see her reception of the tidings, my son. I was quite touched and pleased with the grace with which she spoke of my former kindness, and the joy she should feel in testifying the reality of her gratitude. I can assure you, Friend, the lovers made quite a pretty picture at that moment. You really ought to have been present."

Quitting the room hastily that she might not revel in the evidence of the pain which her malice caused me, I retreated to the library, and sitting down at the table began to muse upon this most curious coincidence. But presently I started to my feet with a dismayed ejaculation.

Facing me was the calendar of the month with the 2nd of June marked upon it.

"The 2nd of June," I muttered; "the 2nd of June, surely it cannot be!"

But the exciting events of the last twenty-four hours had hopelessly confused me. Taking out my pocket diary I turned to the date. There it was, sure enough—"Wednesday, the 2nd of June."

Then, with a smothered cry, I brought my clenched fist down upon the table.

"She knew it, then," I muttered, "and she destroyed the envelope lest it should bear witness against her. That letter did not arrive this afternoon. I see it all now. Two days ago she knew that Ella Maclise was an heiress, and that was the reason she stirred Lucien up to urging me to speak to her. She knew she was rich, but she wished her son to gain the credit of wooing her as a poor dependent girl. Oh pray God that Lucien spoke in ignorance. I pray God that he at least was true to her!"

Yes, the sight of the calendar recalled to me, what otherwise perhaps I should never have remembered, that the London postmark at the back of the Indian letter had been May 31st. Therefore it was evident my mother must have been aware of Ella's wealth for two days. Now I understood her rage when she found the letter in my hands, and also the burning of the compromising envelope.

My first impulse on discovering my mother's duplicity was to question Lucien closely on the subject of the Indian letter; but after a few minutes of earnest reflection I came to the conclusion that for my own peace it would be better to remain in a condition of ignorance than to arrive at an unsatisfactory certainty. For even if I found that Lucien had been in the plot with his mother, it was now too late to do anything.

I could see at a glance how, to a girl of Ella Maclise's temperament, the knowledge of her wealth would make it absolutely incumbent on her to carry out her promise to my brother. Had she been indeed poor, the breaking off the engagement with him would have been a matter of comparative ease.

Therefore, with a still heavier heart, I decided not to interfere, but to endeavour to give my brother the benefit of the doubt; and indeed it did appear to me to be very possible that our mother had concealed her knowledge from both of us, in the fear that with Lucien's weaker nature he might inadvertently bring the secret to light.

On one thing, however, I was firmly resolved, and that was that I would settle the eighty thousand pounds absolutely on Ella, giving her husband no power whatever over it, so that if he had been influenced by mercenary considerations in his offer of marriage, it should be to his interest to treat her gently and kindly in the future.

After my brother's engagement I was less at home than ever, but I noticed, whenever I saw Lucien and Ella together, that her face was very pale and drawn; that her step had lost its elasticity, and that altogether there was an air of weary indifference about her that in her circumstances seemed to have a very pathetic significance. I tried in vain to shut my eyes to this; my only consolation being, and this • a very sorry one, that in time she might grow to love her husband, even though there was no real affection in her heart when she married him.

But if Ella was at this period listless and languid, my mother, on the other hand, was full of bustle and excitement. After repeated urging, Ella had reluctantly consented that the marriage should take place early in October. It was late in July when my mother and Lucien extracted this promise from her, and therefore we had

scanty time to make our preparations for
the event.

One evening a month after this important
matter was settled, my mother followed me
into the library, to which I invariably retreated now when I was not at my club.

" How much does she want? " I muttered to myself, for it had come to be a
plainly recognised fact that, whenever my
mother sought a private interview with
me, a request for money was sure to follow.

At first, as I have said before, she would
give me some lame reason why she needed
this extra money; but as time went on,
and she perceived how absolute her power
over me became, she grew bolder, and
simply stated her wishes, without going
through the farce of excusing herself or
Lucien, on whose account the amounts
were generally claimed.

Whether she spent this money or whether
she hoarded it I had not the least idea, but
I was rather inclined to think that there

was a curiously inconsistent element in her character, and that while she loved the most lavish display there was also something of the miser in her nature.

I came to this apparently contradictory conclusion on one occasion when I entered my mother's boudoir unexpectedly, and found her counting over a large heap of gold coins, which she had evidently just emptied into her lap from a huge cash box. Hastily she pulled a piece of silk which hung on the back of a chair over the contents of her lap, and, muttering something about the lock of the door being defective, feigned to be busily occupied at her escritoir.

From which I gathered that she had taken the cash box from this escritoir, and also that she fancied by locking the door she had secured herself from interruption while she counted over her treasures.

" Well, mother," I said, seeing she hesitated a little in beginning, "what is it?"

" I want some money, Friend."

" There is nothing unusual in that, it

appears to me," I replied drily. " How much ? "

" Well, rather a large sum—five hundred pounds."

I bit my lip, and began to beat an impatient tatoo upon the table. At this time my own expenses were very heavy, and I felt if my mother's demands were likely in the future to assume these serious proportions that my position might become an embarrassed one, even with respect to money.

" It is, as you say, a very large sum," I muttered uneasily.

" Yet, my son, when you understand for what purpose I want it, I fancy you will give it to me willingly."

I looked up at her in surprise, and she continued—

" Friend, I wish to present Ella with her trousseau."

" Her trousseau ! " I exclaimed ; " why I thought you had been busy about that for the last fortnight. It seems to me that whenever I go up or down stairs I meet somebody with a milliner's box."

" Ah, you can't be expected to understand anything of these matters, Friend. The serious business of the trousseau is not commenced yet, and, as I say, I wish to defray the expenses of it. I must have done this, of course, had Ella not succeeded to her uncle's fortune before marrying Lucien ; and now that she is rich I don't want to appear to take advantage of that circumstance. With five hundred pounds I could furnish her with a good trousseau— not an extravagant one—but sufficiently good. I admit I don't feel inclined to spend this money myself, whereas I am quite sure you will be delighted to do the thing generously."

I made no reply until I had written the cheque.

" There," I said, handing it to her, " is a cheque for seven hundred and fifty pounds. Spare no expense, mother, and you will do me a service ; but for Heaven's sake don't let her imagine that I have had any hand in this matter. Let her fancy it is your wedding present."

My mother readily agreed to this, and I thought no more of the subject. A month later, however, when the wedding was only five weeks distant, I was much surprised to be informed by a clerk, as I sat in my private office in the city, that a lady desired to see me.

" A lady ! " I ejaculated in astonishment. " A lady here ! What is her name ? "

" I do not know, sir; but she said she wished to see you particularly."

" Show her in, then. I am at her service."

" A minute later he re-appeared, ushering into the room no less a person than Charlie Hall's pretty wife.

" Julia ! " I cried, running towards her. "Oh, Julia, I am so glad to see you ! "

Here I stopped short. Instead of returning my warm greeting, Julia Hall scarcely touched my hand with hers, and now that I had leisure to observe her, I saw that her eyes flashed and that her lips were firmly and haughtily compressed.

"Why, Julia," I exclaimed in dismay, " have I offended you ? "

"And if you have, I should imagine, by the way you have neglected us lately, that it is not a matter of any consequence to you, Mr. Perditus," she rejoined coldly.

"'Mr. Perditus!'" I echoed. "Well, perhaps I ought not to complain. I know I must have appeared terribly ungrateful to you all."

"Why have you stayed away, then, all this time ? " she asked sharply.

"Because," I faltered, " Charlie seemed angry about something the last time I did come ; and—well, I have stayed away for another reason, which I cannot explain."

"You have no need to explain," she said. " I can imagine your reason very well ; you stayed away because you were ashamed of yourself, Friend Perditus."

"Julia!" I cried, shrinking from her.

Then, to my great consternation, sinking into a chair, Julia Hall covered her face with her hands, and burst into tears.

"Oh, Friend," she sobbed, "it is of no use, I can't keep it up. I can't be angry with you, and you looking so miserably ill, too. Oh, Friend, Friend, why have you done it? We are all so unhappy about it."

"I don't understand you, Julia," I said, much concerned, "but I see that there is something wrong. What is it? Surely you will tell me. Charlie is not in any difficulty, is he?"

"No, and if he were, you wouldn't care," she cried, flashing out again. "You dont care for any of us; you have changed altogether. Mother says so, and we all say so, and I determined to let you know it without Charlie's having any notion of what I intended. I thought it was only acting the part of a friend to open your eyes to what you are doing."

Dropping her aggressive tone, with another burst of tears, she continued—

"Friend, if anybody had told me a year ago that you would play fast and loose with a girl, I would not have believed it. We all thought you the most honourable man we knew."

"What do you mean?" I stammered.

"That you have treated Ella Maclise abominably. First of all you make her love you, and then you throw her over. Oh, it's shameful!"

In great distress I interrupted her.

"Julia," I murmured, "you pain me terribly. Indeed, you should not talk in that way; remember you are speaking of my brother's affianced wife."

"I know I am," she cried passionately, "and that is why I speak. Oh, Friend, listen to me," she continued earnestly, "listen to me while there is time. I know why Ella Maclise consented to marry your brother: it was because she loved you, and felt that her only chance of remaining near you was by becoming his wife."

"If you have any pity, stop!" I gasped. "You do not understand; you are mistaken."

"I am not," she persisted. "Friend, I know I am telling the truth. She loves you! Oh, let me give her one word of consolation. She loves you, and it breaks my heart to see her pale face and wistful eyes. It is not too late even now; break off this match that you have made, and comfort this poor aching heart."

"I cannot, I cannot," I moaned. "Oh, Julia, you have given me my death blow! Why not have left me in peace? surely I have suffered enough?"

The colour faded out of her cheeks.

"But why should you suffer, Friend?" she murmured.

"Listen to me," I said, breathing heavily and speaking hoarsely. "I am the most unhappy man in the world; more unhappy than words can say because I cannot explain the cause of my wretchedness. I love Ella Maclise. I would give my life to save her one pang, but I cannot marry her."

" You cannot ! "

" No, I cannot, though to do so would make this earth a heaven to me."

" Then there is no more for me to say," she murmured sadly, " except to beg your pardon, Friend; I don't know what your trouble is, but I grieve for you from my heart." •

Rising she held out her hand; but, with utter inconsistency, now that she had spoken on the subject, I longed to hear more of her reasons for believing in Ella's love for me.

" Tell me more of her," I moaned out. " Oh, Julia, you do not know what it has been, what it is, to live under the same roof with her, to love her so entirely that I envy the very ground she walks on, and yet to be obliged to shun her sweet society, or when I do see her to scarcely dare to speak lest I should forget the miserable position in which I stand."

Taking my hand in hers, Julia Hall sat down by my side.

"I don't know what I can tell you, Friend, that will not add to your grief," she murmured ; " but when I said Ella had accepted your brother that she might remain near you it was only the truth. I found it out more than a month ago. For some days, in fact ever since she became engaged to Lucien, she had avoided me, but one morning she called to ask if I thought my brother Frank could arrange a little business matter for her. Naturally I was surprised at this, and inquired why she had not applied to you in her difficulty ? Then, Friend, she broke down, and confessed the whole truth to me. It seemed for some time past she had felt she ought to leave Brook Street, that it was undignified to remain your guest when she had evidently offended you in some way, and yet the idea of separating from you broke her heart.

For a time she was almost distracted on
this account; then she noticed a change
in Mrs. Guadella also; and ultimately she
came to the conclusion that she must make
up her mind to one of two things; either to
marry Lucien, or to estrange herself from
your family altogether. She could not do
that, Friend. I don't say she acted rightly,
but I can understand her. Her life would
be empty without you, and so she marries
your brother."

In utter misery I sat silent for a few
minutes, and then I murmured—

"And what was it she wanted Frank to
do for her; does she doubt my friendship,
even ?"

"No, I think not, but she naturally felt
a delicacy in applying to you about her
monetary perplexities."

"Her monetary perplexities ?" I cried.

"Why yes, it seems she is not likely
to receive any of this Indian money for
a year, and she wanted to borrow some, in
fact."

" But what in the world for ? "

" Why, Friend," said Julia, with a faint smile, " is the necessity for a wedding trousseau quite beneath your manly consideration ? "

" No," I answered ; "but why should she borrow for that ? "

" Because such things as a rule cannot be procured without money."

" But," I cried impulsively, " you don't understand. Ella Maclise requires nothing for that purpose ; my mother supplies her with her trousseau."

" Really ? " was the reply, in tones of unfeigned surprise.

" Well," I stammered, " my mother wished to present it to her ; but as she was short of money she came to me for the means, and I gave her seven hundred and fifty pounds for the purpose."

Julia uttered a cry of astonishment, but as she was about to speak she stopped short, and I saw a gleam of anger come into her eyes.

"When did you give this money, Friend?" she asked.

"I don't exactly know," I answered, passing my hand over my brow; "but I can easily find out." Taking my cheque book I turned over the leaves. "Here it is," I said; "I wrote the cheque on the 30th of August."

"Ah," replied Julia drily, "that was four days before Ella called on me. I recollect the date because the 3rd of September happens to be my birthday." •

Hopelessly confused I stared at her.

"It's curious," I murmured; "how do you account for it?"

"Oh, I don't attempt to account for it," she said irritably; "but it's evident your mother had not told Ella of her generous intentions at that time, and," she continued meaningly, "that she wishes her wedding trousseau to be a surprise at the last moment."

"Good Heavens!" I cried, springing to my feet, "that's impossible. You mean that you think my mother never intended," and then I stumbled giddily against the table, and clung tightly to it to prevent myself falling to the ground.

At once Julia's kind, warm heart gushed out.

"Oh, Friend!" she cried, running to me, and helping me to a chair; "Oh, dear Friend, what is the matter? Let me call some one; you are going to faint, I am sure you are?"

"No," I panted, shaking my head and pointing to the window; "open the window please, I shall be better in a minute."

I waited for an instant, during which Julia dabbed my forehead with some stimulating perfume which she had taken from her pocket, and then I murmured—

"You must not be alarmed, Julia; it is nothing of any consequence. I have had several similar attacks lately, and altogether I am out of sorts. I expect it's the excitement and worry I have gone through; but besides this giddiness I have had a most un-

pleasant tingling sensation in my head for
the last two or three weeks."

Very anxiously she looked at me.

"Why not consult Charlie?" she said
earnestly. "Friend, you can't tell the
trouble it has been to all of us, but especially to Charlie and mother, to see so little of
you. Now, do consult Charlie, for you know
it may be something serious."

"I don't care much if it is," I replied
gloomily; and then, seeing that she looked
very shocked, and that her kind eyes filled
with tears, I tried to speak more cheerfully.

"At any rate," I continued, "I have no
time just now to think of myself. I am
furnishing Lucien's home—that is to be my
wedding present to both of them—and I
am also trying to negotiate a junior partner-
ship in this firm for him. He won't draw a
large income out of it for some years, but
the occupation will be good for him, and I
shall find it easier to lend him a helping
hand if we are connected in business. So

you see, Julia, nursing is out of the question
just now; but when all my work is done, I
will doctor myself up; that is if dear old
Charlie still feels sufficient interest in me to
undertake my case."

Taking my hand in hers the warm hearted
girl pressed it affectionately.

"You know, Friend," she murmured,
"there is no one that Charlie loves so well
as you, except me. However coldly you
treated him, I am sure you could not wear
out his patience."

And thereupon, with another pressure of
the hand, she left me.

CHAPTER XIII

But though I made light of my condition
to Julia Hall, in reality for two or three
weeks past I had considered it very serious.
Three or four times in the day these alarm-
ing attacks of giddiness would seize me;
but what appeared to me more important,
because less ordinary than the actual attack
itself, was the very peculiar sensation which
almost invariably preceded it.

This sensation it is very difficult for me
to convey an adequate impression of.

Suddenly, without any preparation, there
would come upon me an overwhelming
presentiment of something being about to
happen, an almost painful sense of expectancy, in fact; but when I seemed to be
positively on the brink of some discovery—

what, I could not tell—with a crash the dizziness would descend upon me, blotting everything out, and leaving me in a condition of such utter exhaustion, that, completely prostrated, I would be obliged to remain quite quiet for an hour at least after the attack.

As the time for the wedding drew nearer, these seizures became more frequent, and I began to be seriously afraid that, after all, I should not be able to complete the business I had in hand before I succumbed to the illness with which I felt sure I must be threatened.

I absented myself more than ever from my home, for I was aware that in the society of Ella Maclise my malady became more pronounced; in fact, it seemed to me anything that stirred me to deep emotion increased my ailment, and I could not look upon her sad face, which each day grew paler and more wan, without so sickening a sense of bitter regret and self-reproach that my heart would flutter and my brain throb until a cold dread came upon me as to whether my strange sensations could be the premonitory symptoms of madness. And then I would clasp my hands and pray that my reason might be spared to me at least until I had done Ella Maclise some scant justice.

This dread came upon me very forcibly one day about a week before the 5th of October, the day upon which my darling was to become my brother's wife.

Ella had received a box from India, containing a variety of curios which had been discovered in her uncle's house after his decease, and to which, as sole heiress, she was entitled. In the midst of the box containing these things was a smaller one, which, from an explanatory note, she found was an offering from the gentleman who acted as her uncle's executor, and contained some peculiar aromatic Indian perfumes, and some sweetmeats and conserves of native manufacture.

We were in the dining-room when this

box arrived, and by mutual consent, when the lid had been wrenched off by the servants, the whole thing was lifted bodily on to the table, that the ladies, assisted by Lucien, might rummage among its contents to their heart's desire.

While this was going forward I stood, as usual, in the background; but presently I became conscious of a sickly sweet odour which seemed strangely familiar to me, and at once the curious sensation of expectancy began to steal over me. Involuntarily I advanced, and saw that Ella held in her hand a beautifully inlaid casket of the most delicate Indian work.

"What is it?" I panted, for the subtle aroma seemed to stifle me.

"Some sort of sweetmeat, I believe," she answered, not looking at me. Alas, we never dared to look into each other's eyes now! "Will you take one?"

I stretched out my hand, but as I did so the ground began to rock under my feet, and I knew that I had arrived at the second stage of my mysterious malady.

With a muttered excuse I staggered out of the room, for of all things I dreaded succumbing to the awful exhaustion which always succeeded the giddiness, before Ella. Holding on to the wall and anything that stood in my way, I managed to reach the library, and there I flung myself down upon the sofa, and for an hour or more I moved neither hand nor foot.

Wearily, heavily, the week dragged on, and each morning when I awoke I murmured to myself—

" It is one day nearer ; shall I live to see the day, I wonder ? "

And then I would bathe my aching, throbbing head, and try to persuade myself that the strange tingling sensation, which never left me now, was perhaps a trifle better, and that the dull booming sound in my ears was not of any serious importance.

I breakfasted now by myself, pretending

that an accession of business necessitated my being at my office at an unusually early hour; the truth being that a glimpse of Ella's unhappy face was sufficient to unman me completely; and therefore, with the day's work before me, I dared not meet her.

The misery that I suffered no words can describe. Until my conversation with Julia Hall there had been a possibility in my mind—though, I admit, a very very faint possibility—that Ella's love for me had not survived my coldness to her; but now this merciful doubt, to which I had clung desperately, was torn from me, and in addition to my own burden of unatoned guilt and remorse, I had to bear that of knowing I had wrecked the happiness and desolated the heart of the woman I loved beyond all words.

I knew that her marriage with my brother would be a sacrilege in the eyes of God; but what could I do? Was it not part of the punishment that had been appointed to me? I judged her feelings by my own, and haunted by her pale face and wistful eyes I did not dare to interfere; for I knew that immeasurably beyond all other sorrows to her would be the sorrow of recognising the utter unworthiness and baseness of the one to whom she had given her heart. I idolised and worshipped her; to have thrown down the image of ideal purity that I had set up, and before my eyes to have broken and bespattered it, would have been a greater torment even than those under which I now shuddered and groaned, and knowing that she believed as completely in me, would any other man in my miserable position have unmasked himself before her? And yet it seems to me that only in that way could I have hoped to prevent her marriage.

On the morning of the 4th of October I was conscious that my symptoms were certainly intensified, and, shivering with apprehension, I thought of the day's programme that I had laid down for myself. At noon I was to accompany my brother and his affianced wife to the house in South Hampstead that I had been furnishing for them, to ascertain if anything were wanting in the arrangements, that I might get them completed while the bride and bridegroom were on their wedding tour in Scotland; and in the evening there was to be a little gathering at our house, to which Frank Nesbit, Charlie Hall and his wife, and my two young partners had been invited.

For the wedding breakfast and ceremony my mother had sent out invitations broadcast, notwithstanding my most urgent appeals; but this evening had been set apart for business, and therefore Julia Hall was the only outsider that had been asked.

The guests were all assembled in the drawing-room when I descended, and even then I feared that my unsteady gait would attract attention. I had managed to get through the hour in the house in South Hampstead without breaking down, but I was only just able to reach my room before

I succumbed altogether, and so prolonged was this attack and the succeeding faintness and languor, that I began to fear I should not be able to put in an appearance at all, and yet I knew that none of the important business for which we were gathered together could possibly be transacted without my being present.

Stammering my excuses, I shook hands with each of my friends, but when I came to Charlie I stumbled, and should have fallen had he not grasped my arm firmly. •

"My dear boy," he murmured, his kind eyes distended with anxiety. "Why, Friend, what in Heaven's name is the matter with you, old fellow?"

"Nothing," I gasped, "at least nothing I can explain now, but we will have a talk to-morrow evening when everything is quiet. I'm fagged out, that's what it is, Charlie."

Here my mother came up to us.

"Friend," she muttered harshly, 'for goodness sake go and take a nip of brandy or something, you look positively ghastly."

I blinked my burning eyes at her, but I could not see her plainly; in fact everything, even perfectly inanimate objects, appeared to rock up and down, and to advance and suddenly retreat again, in the most perplexing fashion.

" No," I murmured, holding on to Charlie's arm, " I will drink nothing, my brain seems ready to burst already ; but, Charlie, do me a favour, and bring the others after me to the library; I am pretty well done up to-night."

In less than an hour the business was completed; Lucien had been admitted into our firm as junior partner, and afterwards, in the presence of Charlie Hall and my brother, Frank Nesbit drew out the deed by which I settled on Ella, wife of Lucien Guadella, the sum of eighty thousand pounds. The money to be tied up strictly, and to descend to her children if she should have any.

Fortunately I had explained my wishes to Frank Nesbit beforehand, and there was little for me to do except to affix my signature, and to request those present not to inform my future sister-in-law of this settlement in her favour until after the ceremony on the next day. But even in speaking these few words my voice wavered and fluctuated strangely, while as for my signature, the writing was perfectly unrecognisable even to me, so terribly shaky was it.

When it was all over I pulled Lucien apart.

"Take them away, Lucien," I panted, "I must rest for a little while. Tell my friends I am not quite the thing. Call me when supper is ready, I wish to drink the health of the new partner. God bless you, brother, God bless you."

My face was scarcely whiter than his, as without a word he wrung my hand hard and left me alone.

How long a time elapsed before a knock

came to the library door I have not the
least idea. Thinking over the events of
that memorable evening now, it seems to
me that I spent days in the dreamy reverie
in which I was enveloped.

Sitting in my easy chair, with my
throbbing head clasped in my hand, I appeared to be the central figure of a moving
drama, in which, however, I had no part,
and which as it progressed was utterly
independent of any mental effort of my
own.

I knew that the light in my room
was very dim, for when the others had left
me I lowered the lamp to ease my burning
eyes, and yet on every side of me there
appeared to be an immense glow of ruddy
sunlight; and while in reality the weather
was cold and chilly, the air seemed to me so
sultry that I was tempted to unbutton the
stiff collar of my dress shirt.

And again, I was perfectly aware that I
was alone, and yet in front of me, and
on each side of me, there flitted white-

robed turbaned figures with dusky faces and glittering teeth and eyeballs.

More than once I rose and shook myself, and then the figures faded away into obscurity, and I was myself once more; but soon they returned, and by their mysterious movements lulled me again into the land of dreams.

Presently, however, the knock at my door interrupted me, and at the sound, as though affrighted, the visions shrank away.

With a desperate effort I pulled myself together and followed the servant.

How I reached my chair at the head of the table I don't know, but I fancied at the time, that, as I stumbled giddily forward, one of the white-robed figures came to my side and assisted me.

I imagine that I sat down, but I neither ate nor drank, and I know that I could not have spoken, for my tongue clave to the roof of my mouth, and the air seemed loaded to the point of suffocation with faint odours.

I heard the hum of voices on all sides of me, but I could not distinguish any faces except the dusky faces which had surrounded me in the other room.

"What does it mean," I muttered to myself. "Oh, God, what does it mean? Is this madness?"

And then I stretched out my hand blindly towards my plate. In my bewilderment it occurred to me that perhaps if I ate something the spell which was upon me might loosen.

In front of me was a little glass dish; what it contained I had not the slightest notion, but I perceived dimly that it was full of small dark objects, and, entirely heedless of appearances, I took one of these in my fingers, and lifted it towards my mouth.

It was evidently a sweetmeat with a strongly aromatic odour.

As the subtle scent penetrated my nostrils, at once my heart gave an awful bound, and then began to throb and leap wildly within

my breast in the manner that I knew so
well.

"It is coming," I panted under my
breath. "This time it is surely coming to
me, but what? Oh, God in Heaven
what?"

I placed the sweetmeat in my mouth and
then——Heaven only knows what happened.
I seemed to hear a terrific crash, which for
the moment stunned me completely, but
suddenly the thick darkness which enveloped me appeared to roll away, and I
saw clearly and distinctly.

With a scream I sprang to my feet and
looked around.

One moment I glared at the shrinking
terrified group, and then, dashing my chair
to the ground I rushed to the other end of
the table, striking right and left at those
who would have impeded my progress.

"Give way, give way!" I shrieked. "He
has escaped me twice, but never again!
Thank Heaven, never again!"

And then, before I could be prevented, I

hurled myself upon the cowering, trembling figure of Lucien Guadella.

"I know you now!" I yelled. "Oh, my enemy, I know you now! Lucien Guadella! false friend, coward and thief! My hand is at your throat! Beg no mercy from me, for I will show none!"

With herculean strength I grasped him, but suddenly my power deserted me, my fingers relaxed, and with a moan I fell heavily to the ground.

  * * * * *

We are told by those who narrowly escape death by drowning, that in an inconceivably short space of time the events of a long life will arise before the mental vision in a series of dramatic scenes, and I can well understand it now, since as I fell the curtain which had concealed my former life from me ascended, and these were the scenes which were severally presented to my view.

CHAPTER XIV

In a darkened room in Calcutta sits a widowed lady with a pale refined face and prematurely white hair. On a rug at her feet, leaning up against her knees, with one of her thin fragile hands clasped in his, is a stalwart fair-haired lad of seventeen years. As the curtain ascends, it is the lad who speaks.

"Mother," he says very earnestly, "you must not grieve on my account. I will not deny that if I could have had my choice I would have followed my father's profession—the Sherwoods have been soldiers for many generations—but that is clearly impossible. Therefore, let us look on the bright side of things, and be sure of this, dear, a banker's clerk may be as chivalrous a gentleman as the commander-in-chief himself."

*   *   *   *   *

The next scene is a sadder one. The lad is now a man of twenty-three, but the widow lies upon her death-bed, with her head pillowed upon her son's breast.

"God bless you, John," she pants, while the dews gather upon her forehead quicker than with all his tenderness he can wipe them away. "God bless my dear son, the best, the truest friend that ever a mother had. Not one moment's sorrow have you ever caused me, John. Your father and I will wait at heaven's gate for our darling; be sure of that."

*   *   *   *   *

Again the scene changes.

On a wicker sofa on a verandah lounges John Sherwood. He has a cigar between his teeth, and an open novel in his hand; but the evening is intensely sultry, and notwithstanding the draught of air from a punkah near, which is being worked by a patient figure in white, the young man is restless and ill at ease.

"This is the effect of last night's dissipation, I suppose," he mutters to himself; "I thought I should never get through my work to-day. Those Guadella's are queer people, I fancy, though there's something undeniably attractive about Lucien. He seems to have seen such a lot of the world, and yet he can't be as old as I am by several years. Well, there are very few men of five-and-twenty who have travelled as little as I have. I shall not go to their house often, for the mother's such an awful caution with her theatrical get-up and music hall songs; but I hope the son will look me up, for he amuses me, and the monotony of my life begins to pall upon me a bit."

* * * * *

Once more the curtain rises.

Six months have elapsed. In the private room of Mr. Foley, the manager of Manton's

bank, sits John Sherwood.   His face is very
white, and his attitude is one of utter dejec-
tion, as, resting his chin on his hand, he
stares through the partially-closed venetian
shutters of the window at the little patch of
sunburnt grass which is in the centre of the
walled courtyard at the back of the bank.

" I have been a fool," he mutters, through
his closed teeth, " a weak fool, but perhaps
it is as well that my betting and gambling
have turned out so badly ; success might
have encouraged me to persevere. As it is, I
am cleaned out altogether. Poor mother,
I hope she doesn't know into whose pockets
all my little savings have gone. I wonder
how Guadella got on last night ? badly,
I expect. Well, it is no use his coming
to me to-day ; I haven't got a rupee to
bless myself with. Luckily to-morrow's
pay day, or I should have had to ask for
an advance, and I wouldn't do that for the
world. If the firm knew I had been seen
gambling, it would shake their confidence
in me seriously."

With a sigh John Sherwood rises and walks towards the open window. Opening a locket which hangs at his watch-chain, he presses his lips to a miniature of his mother.

"Mother," he whispers, "I thank God that I have received this shock, for it has cured me of an infatuation. I have gambled for the last time. I promise you, with Heaven's help, in future I will be worthy of my father's memory and of yours."

The door of the room opens.

"A gentleman, Mr. Maclise, on private business, Mr. Sherwood."

"Show him in."

Mr. Maclise is a white-haired man with an unusually florid countenance and short thick throat. At once he commences his business.

"You are Mr. Foley's head clerk, I believe?" he says shortly and incisively.

"In the absence of my senior, Mr. Morgan, who is away on his holiday, I am, sir," John Sherwood replies.

u 2

Mr. Maclise nods, and takes from his pocket a leathern case.

" In this case," he says, " are sixty unset diamonds. They are worth, at least forty thousand pounds. I am leaving Calcutta in two days, but meanwhile I have been advised by Mr. Foley to deposit them here."

" Mr. Foley has not yet arrived, and I don't expect him until the afternoon, shortly before the bank closes," murmurs John Sherwood.

" Ah, I understood from him yesterday that I should not be likely to see him ; but he told me to give my property into the hands of John Sherwood, in whom he has unbounded confidence, and who has a duplicate key of his safe. You are John Sherwood, I suppose ? "

" Certainly ; and since those are Mr. Foley's wishes, I will give you a receipt at once, and put the stones into the safe immediately."

He writes the slip of paper, and, taking his bunch of keys from his pocket, opens

the ponderous safe, which is built into a
recess in the wall. Depositing the diamonds
therein, he re-locks the safe, and then Mr.
Maclise takes his hat off the table and
prepares to depart.

" Good morning to you, Mr. Sherwood,"
he says pleasantly, holding out his hand,
" I feel decidedly more comfortable in my
mind now. I lay awake all last night with
a revolver under my pillow. Hotels, and
especially Indian hotels, where so much
ventilation is absolutely necessary, don't
give you any great notion of security.
Why, the very idea of anything going
wrong with those diamonds makes me
shudder. I can tell you, when a man has
a little daughter to provide for, these things
assume very important proportions."

As Mr. Maclise shuts the door after him,
John Sherwood passes his hand wearily over
his forehead.

" Confound it," he mutters, with a sigh,
" how my head aches ; and no wonder. My
conscience pricked me sorely when that old

fellow talked about Mr. Foley's unbounded confidence in me. I wonder what he would say if he knew that yesterday I had been obliged to draw out every farthing of my savings and pay it away to that blackguard Smith? I wish now I hadn't told young Donald about it, in case it gets to the governor's ears; but it came out in spite of me, and I don't suppose he will break confidence."

" By Jove ! " he exclaims, stopping short, " my head must be in a pretty state of confusion this morning! If I haven't given Mr. Maclise a receipt for sixty diamonds without counting the stones to make sure the number is correct! I must be a fool, indeed; a nice, reliable sort of person to leave in charge ! "

Grumbling at himself, John Sherwood unlocks the safe once more, and taking out the leathern case seats himself with his back towards the window.

But for this slight circumstance all his after miseries might have been spared him.

As it is, he spreads the glittering diamonds out upon the wash-leather in front of him, and has almost finished counting them before he becomes aware that his proceedings are being closely watched through the venetian blinds behind him.

At last, however, a slight sound startles him, and then, glancing quickly over his shoulder, he springs to his feet with a cry of alarm.

"All right, Sherwood," a voice whispers to him; "it's only me. Is the coast clear?"

Greatly surprised, John Sherwood approaches the window.

"Guadella," he cries, "why, how in the name of wonder did you get here?"

"Over the wall," the other whispers. "The next premises are empty and join the road. I am a famous climber, and I managed it easily."

"But why didn't you come in the front way and ask for me?" inquires John.

"Because, from what you said last night,

I fancied you didn't want your intimacy with me to get to the ears of the governor. I knew you would be alone here—you told me so. I wanted to ask you a favour, and as I am not proud I preferred slipping in by the back way to compromising my friend in the eyes of his respectable employers."

"Nevertheless you should not have done so, Lucien," replies the other uneasily; "if anyone had seen you scaling that wall it would have looked awfully suspicious."

"Oh, you make you mind quite comfortable; there are not many people about at this time of the morning. Why, it's only just past ten. At any rate I took good care nobody should see me, and I shall depart in the same way, when you've fulfilled my little request. Here, stop a minute, let's have a glance at those stones. Seen through the blind, you looked a thorough-going miser counting over his treasures."

"I can't show you them, Guadella; it's against the rules," murmurs Sherwood hurriedly, placing them in the safe and locking the door. "They have been deposited here this morning."

" With you ? " inquires the other eagerly.

" Well, through me; I have given the receipt," Sherwood replies.

There is a momentary silence, during which Guadella looks carelessly round the room. All at once he gives an evident start, and then with his white hand covering his mouth, which begins to twitch nervously, he says—

" Sherwood, I have scarcely a minute to spare, but I'm in an awful mess this morning. Can you help me ? "

John Sherwood shrugs his shoulders rather hopelessly.

" What is it ? " he asks.

" It's just this. You know how often you've urged me to try and get something to do ? "

Sherwood nods.

" Well, this morning I've heard of a berth in a merchant's office. Not much at first, but a prospect of rising."

" I congratulate you, Guadella."

" No, don't do that, prematurely. Now the hole I'm in is this :—Following your example, I too got cleaned out last night; and worse than cleaned out, for I owe one of the fellows twenty pounds. Now, unless I can pay this money this morning the brute threatens to go and tell my new governor, and then of course it's all up with me."

" By George! That's a serious matter ! " exclaims Sherwood sympathetically.

" Horribly serious unless you can lend me the twenty pounds until brighter days."

" But my dear fellow I haven't a penny, you know that."

" But you will have, to-morrow."

" Yes, I get my quarter's salary of a hundred pounds to-morrow. I'll lend it you then gladly, Guadella."

" But that will be too late," urged the other.

" But I can do nothing else."

" Yes, you can, you can get young Donald to let you have the money now at once ; the chap got his uncle's little legacy cashed yesterday. I know his pockets are bulging with coin to-day."

" I know that, too," John replies. " I gave him a little good advice by the light of my own experience this morning."

" Well, for Heaven's sake borrow twenty pounds of him, and get me out of this terrible hole. You can pay him to-morrow. He's in the outer office, I'll wait here until you come back. Come, Sherwood, it's not like a friend to let a fellow sink for want of a helping hand."

Terribly perplexed, for a minute Sherwood stands irresolute.

" I'll try Donald, Guadella," he says at length, " but I am doing for you what I really wouldn't do for myself."

" Don't hurry, my dear fellow, it's cool in here, and your gov'nor isn't likely to come and find me."

When Sherwood gets into the outer office a variety of things occur to detain him, and quite twenty minutes elapse before he finds an opportunity of speaking privately to Donald. This young man makes no difficulty about the matter, but hands him over the twenty pounds in gold at once; with this John returns to the private room, wondering whether Guadella's patience is quite exhausted; his wonder increases, however, when he finds the room empty.

"I am sorry," he murmurs. "I suppose the noise in the outer office made him nervous; however, very likely he will be back soon, if not I must try and find him at lunch time. I should be truly grieved if he missed this chance, for I like him notwithstanding that I can't feel he's absolutely straight. But then any fellow is handicapped with such a mother as that. He might do well in the world if he had a chance. Well, I hope he will, I'm sure, for of all the unpleasant offices of friendship I have ever performed borrowing that twenty pounds was the worst."

He seats himself, and for more than an

hour he works with a will. Presently, however, he rises to fetch something he requires from the outer office; as he leaves the table he utters a short cry of dismay.

"Good Heavens!" he exclaims, "it's lucky for me nobody has come in, or I should get reported to a certainty. Why, I would have sworn I locked that safe when I left the room."

Hastily approaching it he pulls the heavy door towards him.

"Ah," he murmurs in great vexation, "I did lock it, but the door evidently wasn't shut; that's what comes of being in a hurry. Well, if my luck were not greater than my deserts, somebody would have come in, and discovered my carelessness."

Perfectly unsuspiciously he looks into the safe; but after inspecting its contents for an instant a smothered cry breaks from him. In an agony of apprehension he searches the safe from corner to corner, and then with an ashen face and trembling limbs he shuts the heavy door, and leans panting against it.

Horror of horrors! The leathern case containing the diamonds has disappeared!

For a minute or two he seems utterly bewildered by the enormity of his misfortune, and glares wildly about him; but presently a new light comes into his eyes and an exclamation of ungovernable rage bursts from him.

"It is Guadella!" he cries in smothered accents, clenching his fists. "This explains his anxiety to get rid of me; he noticed that I had not secured the door; he has robbed the bank, and ruined me! Oh, merciful Heaven, who will believe in my innocence now?"

Tearing his watch from his pocket he finds that it is a quarter past eleven.

"He has an hour's start only," he mutters desperately, scarcely able with his shaking fingers to lock the safe again. "An hour's start will not save him from me!" And then pulling his hat over his brow to conceal his ghastly face, John

Sherwood passes through the outer office, and, gaining the glaring street, breaks into a swift run.

An hour and a half later the distracted John Sherwood rushes on to the landing stage. The perspiration pours down his white face, and his eyes burn with a feverish maddened glare. He has been to Guadella's home, he has seen his mother, and in an agony of excitement has striven to force the truth from her; but she will tell him nothing of her son except that he has already left Calcutta.

Once more he emerges into the burning sunlight, and controlling himself by a desperate effort, inquires with the utmost caution he can summon to his aid if any one has seen Lucien Guadella. At length he finds that an hour previously he was observed proceeding in the direction of the landing stage, followed by a native porter connected with one of the steamers, bearing a heavy trunk.

But when the well-nigh fainting man

reaches the same spot, the steamer has started, and he recognises that his own ruin is complete.

His brain is bewildered and confused with heat and agitation, but he sees clearly that he cannot hope to establish his innocence. No one knows of Guadella's visit to the bank, but if he alludes to it, it will be thought either that Guadella in his accomplice, or that he is trying to throw his own guilt on to the shoulders of another. No, his only chance of recovering the confidence of honest men and escaping a disgraceful punishment is by regaining possession of the stolen jewels, and to do this he must follow Guadella. But how? How? It must be done at once if it is to be done at all, for already the theft may have been discovered, and the police be on his track.

In this terrible perplexity he meets the master of a small merchant vessel, who was started in life by John Sherwood's grandfather. To him the miserable young man confides his awful position; and, fired by a generous desire to repay some of his old debt of gratitude, this man, now well to do in the world, proposes his vessel as a means of pursuit. No time is lost; all is bustle and activity. Within an hour the small steamer, the " Rose Marie," steams fussily away, and she is scarcely out of sight when the pursuers arrive upon the scene.

From place to place, disguised as one of the crew of the " Rose Marie"—for until he has the jewels or their worth in his possession he dares not confess his own identity—John Sherwood follows Guadella. The skipper, in eager friendship, gives himself up to his service altogether, and the vessel is at his command.

Six weary months pass in this way, and then, in Cape Town, the moment arrives, and he is able to place his strong hand on the shoulder of the panic-stricken wretch, and demand the restitution of the stolen property.

The abject creature attempts no resist-
ance. In the first place he delivers up to
the avenger the jewels which he has upon
his person — forty diamonds out of the
original sixty—and then he writes a full
confession of his guilt.

When this is in his possession John Sherwood feels himself justified in promising
Guadella that if he will restore the re-
mainder of the property he will suffer him
to escape from justice.

(It must be understood that Sherwood was
not aware of the result of the robbery. He
did not know of Mr. Maclise's death, and he
ran the risk of incurring blame himself
sooner than have upon his conscience the
burden of delivering up to no doubt well-
deserved punishment, a man whom he had
once regarded with affection.)

Guadella agrees to this with many protes-
tations of his own unworthiness and his
gratitude for the other's clemency; and,
after writing the confession, invites John
Sherwood to accompany him to the place at

which he is staying, that he may deliver up to him the rest of the stolen property.

Unwarily John Sherwood follows him, after leaving the jewels and confession in the safe keeping of the master of the merchant vessel; but five minutes after he has entered Guadella's room his enemy emerges again and locks the door after him, leaving John lying at full length on the hearth-rug with a chloroformed handkerchief over his mouth.

Once more the fierce pursuit commences. This time Guadella need hope for no mercy. Sherwood's brain is on fire.

The quarry flies to England, but close upon his heels follows the furious and despairing man.

The "Rose Marie" makes good speed, and ere the coast of England looms mistily through the gathering shadows she sights the steamship "Hyperion," within whose bulwarks is the fugitive wretch Lucien Guadella.

But in the night time the storm arises,

the terrible storm that will live in men's minds for many a long year, the storm in which three gallant vessels met their doom.

The "Hyperion" comes safely into port; but within a mile of the land the "Rose Marie" is wrecked, and all hands lost with the exception of one man, who is rescued by fishermen and conveyed to the little country hospital.

Lucien Guadella is safe for the present, for the confession of his guilt lies at the bottom of the ocean, and his pursuer knows neither himself nor his enemy.

*   *   *   *   *

CHAPTER XV

I HAVE little more to tell, and yet I would fain linger over the delightful moments which succeeded my recovery from my swoon.

Two days I remained unconscious, and when I opened my eyes I found myself in my dressing-gown lying upon my bed. A fire burnt in the grate, but twilight had fallen, and I could see but dimly.

At the first moment I imagined that I was alone, but as I prepared to raise myself upon my elbow to make sure of this, I heard a movement and a soft smothered exclamation at the head of my bed.

Keeping perfectly still, I waited; and then a slight figure bent over me, and a

pair of anxious eyes gazed steadfastly and
yearningly into mine.

"Do you know me?" a sweet voice
murmured breathlessly. "Oh, Friend, for
Heaven's sake tell me that you know me,
or my heart will break."

"Ella, Ella!" I cried, stretching out my
arms, "what does this mean? Oh, why
am I lying here?"

And then of a sudden the whole truth
flashed across me. Catching her hand in
both of mine, I clung to it.

"You are not married?" I panted;
"don't tell me that, or you will kill me at
once. You have not married him?"

She tried to withdraw her hand, but I
would not loosen my grasp.

"Speak, speak," I implored; "you are
torturing me. Oh, my darling, speak!"

But there was no need for words; the
little hand ceased its struggles, and the
tender eyes were raised to mine.

For one ineffable moment we gazed into
each other's faces with speechless rapture,

and then I knew that the greatest happiness that can come to any man had been vouchsafed to me.

With an inarticulate murmur of thankfulness and love I drew her to me—closer—closer—until the dear head rested upon my breast ; and then, pressing my lips to the soft golden hair, I lifted up my soul in inexpressible joy and gratitude, and was silent.

In the evening I was considered strong enough and sufficiently composed to come down stairs, and then Charlie told me quietly the events that had happened during the time I lay unconscious.

For more than an hour after my attack, it seemed that everything had been in a state of wild confusion. Charlie Hall and his wife and brother-in-law took me under their charge at once, and Ella Maclise, who appeared in a condition bordering on distraction, also devoted herself to my service.

I was placed upon the sofa in the library, and there every means that Charles Hall could think of were taken for my recovery

—but in vain. At last, when more than an hour had elapsed since my attack, and still my faint continued obstinate, Charles Hall determined to telegraph for Dr. Marion, and also to get the advice of one of the principal London physicians.

Frank Nesbit offered to dispatch the telegram and fetch the London doctor; and so intensely anxious was he on my account that not until afterwards did he perceive the full force of the singularity of his having caught a momentary glimpse of Lucien Guadella in a great coat and slouch hat, with a heavy black bag in his hand.

When he returned, however, and there was nothing for any one to do except to await the arrival of the London doctor with what patience they could summon to their aid, this curious proceeding on Guadella's part recurred to him; and mentioning the matter to Charles Hall it was ascertained that neither mother nor son had been spoken with since the moment of my seizure.

Hastily Frank Nesbit left the room to

inquire among the frightened servants, but none of them could tell anything of either of the Guadellas.

At once the house was searched, but there was no sign of them. In the boudoir, however, the escritoir stood wide open, and from the wardrobe of this terrible woman the jewel-case had disappeared.

No further explanation of Mrs. Guadella's continued demands for money, or of the mysteries connected with the imitation diamond necklace, the outrageous suite of drawing-room furniture, and Ella's trousseau, was necessary now. It was evident that this pair of impostors had been putting by money from the first, that in case my recovery should ever come about they would have the means of supporting themselves in the future. I imagine when they fled from the house in which they had been sheltered for more than a year that they must have carried with them close upon six thousand pounds in notes and money, besides the diamond necklace.

Frank Nesbit gave information to the police that night; but on the morning following my recovery, still weak but unutterably happy, with my dear love by my side, I drove to Scotland Yard, and ordered that all proceedings should be stopped.

I know that I was weak in this, and that this miserable pair of sinners deserved as heavy a punishment as the law could bestow upon them; but my heart was so full of the joy of the present, and I seemed to be imbued with the power of shaking off so completely the shadow of my sufferings in the past, that I could not recognise a sense of personal injury.

As I said to Frank Nesbit, a week afterwards, when he expostulated with me on this point—

"My dear fellow, I am perfectly content, and for that to some extent I have to thank the Guadellas. No man can appreciate happiness to the full who has not known absolute misery. Therefore, if I pursue these criminals, it must be in a spirit of revenge, and how can you expect a man who is in a perfect dream of bliss to make any endeavour to rouse up such a fell sprite as the demon of vengeance? Frank, I have everything that mortal man can wish for now; the love of my darling, the honoured memory of my dear mother— ah, who can imagine the rapture of that thought! a clear conscience, the kindest, truest friends in the world, and perfect health; you yourself heard what Dr. Marion said, that my recovery was absolute and complete. Ah, my boy, let me forget the past, and leave these unhappy wretches to be punished or not, as God wills."

Ella and I were married within a month —Charlie Hall, his wife, Frank, his dear mother and wife, and Dr. Marion alone being present. Our wedding was a very unostentatious one, but all the happier I believe on that account; at any rate I am certain of this; as we drove away that after- noon, leaving our friends standing in a group on the steps of the house, with their

tender farewells still sounding in my ears
and Ella's hand clasped in mine, no man
was ever prouder, more blest, or more at
peace than I.

After a week in Winchester we started
for India. I was anxious to retrieve my
character there; and moreover I desired
to get out of England until the nine days'
wonder of my peculiar illness, and the discovery of the Guadellas' fraud upon me,
should have had time to blow over.

Before I started, however, I had the
doubtful pleasure of reading a long article
on my extraordinary case which some one
had sent to the "Lancet," who, I never
found out, but I rather suspected Harry
Nesbit, who was rapidly developing into a
very enthusiastic young medico.

The article stirred up quite a contro-
versy on the vexed question of suspended
memories; but I do not fancy any clearer
conclusion has been arrived at on this
intricate subject in consequence. The
generally accepted belief in my case ap-

peared to be, that in my recovery the theory of the senses of taste and smell being stronger than any other, where memory is concerned, was very plainly demonstrated.

I, however, am not quite a convert to this idea, though naturally I cannot pretend to any definite opinion on the matter. But I am inclined to think myself that, whether I had eaten that sweetmeat or not, the same thing would have occurred. I fancy I had been working up to this climax for some time past, and that it was only a coincidence that the denouement came at the exact moment it did. However, I suppose no one can decide upon such a point, and I must admit I was glad when another and more extraordinary case of something else, distracted the attention of the medical profession from me.

In India I had little difficulty in establishing my innocence, and I was quite touched at the delight of Mr. Foley and my old companions at the bank when it was officially declared that no shadow any longer rested upon the name of John Sherwood.

But since there remained no one of my family, since I found that I was, in fact, the last of the Sherwoods, I resolved that I would still continue to bear the name I had chosen for myself. It had grown dear to me, and my darling feeling the same, to the end of my life I shall be known as "Friend Perditus."

It was a melancholy pleasure to me before leaving India to make a provision for the widow and child of the master of the "Rose Marie," who had been so staunch a friend to me in my trouble, and also to visit my mother's grave.

I have been married two years now, and surely I may believe that the happiness of my present existence is destined to be permanent. I do not expect, nor do I hope, to go through life without troubles, for it seems to me troubles, if they are not of too overwhelming a nature, keep our sympathies on the alert. I know, too, that

I have no cause to fear trouble, for any
that crosses my path will be lightened and
rendered bearable through the bond of perfect sympathy that exists between me and
my sweet wife, who each day becomes dearer
and dearer to my heart.

Three months ago, it is true, a shadow
fell across my path—a black shadow, re-
calling to me days and nights of bitter
agony, but it has passed away now, and in
its passing how clearly the hand of God and
the all-pervading justice of Providence can
be recognised.

Charles Hall and I had been spending a
few days together in Paris. Charlie had
been overworked and anxious about some
important cases, and on the recovery of his
patients our two wives had urged our going
away together for a little bachelor outing.

The last evening of our stay in Paris had
arrived, and we were sauntering by the door
of one of the minor *café chantants*, when a
highly-coloured picture of a two-headed
singer, or some such unpleasant and pitiable

freak of nature, caught Charlie's eye. Such spectacles are to me extremely disagreeable and depressing, but Charlie appeared to wish to satisfy his scientific curiosity on the subject, and therefore I suppressed all mention of my own feelings, and followed him into the place.

As we entered, on all sides we heard a hubbub of angry voices, which almost drowned the feeble efforts of a female singer who was invisible to us from where we stood. The audience was composed almost exclusively of the lower order, and, as the singer persevered, each minute their remarks became more insultingly contemptuous, and their gesticulations of disgust more violent.

"Ah, but she is ugly !   She is old ! "

"Let us hiss her."

"What do they mean by permitting the old wretch to appear before us ? "

"Throw something at her ; get rid of her."

My blood began to boil, and I clenched

my fists. I could not see the singer, but
to hear men taunting and deriding a woman
was hard to bear, and a feeble woman
evidently, judging from her voice, which
quavered pitiably.

Presently a more than usually cracked
note fell upon our ears, and, immediately a
shriek of derisive laughter came from the
crowded audience. Hands were raised on
every side, and a shower of missiles, most of
them harmless it is true, cakes, and balls of
paper, were projected at the unfortunate
singer.

Still she struggled bravely on, but while
I was wondering at the strength of her
courage, of a sudden I heard a piercing
shriek, and then the smash of a glass.

" The brutes ! " I shouted, pushing my
way through the murmuring crowd, " they
have thrown a glass at her. They have
injured her ! Here make way, you French
cowards, don't let me see one of you lift a
hand again or you'll feel the weight of an
Englishman's fist."

Fortunately the bystanders did not understand my insulting words, or Charlie and I
would have had our work cut out for us, I
expect; still, men that could bully a woman
are not very formidable adversaries, after all.

The people did not oppose our progress,
and in less than two minutes we were in
front of the platform upon which the
trembling singer stood, leaning against a
table, with a blood-stained handkerchief
concealing her face.

In an instant I had climbed upon the
stage, Charlie following close behind; but
as I reached the woman she sank moaning
on the floor in a heap, still with her face
covered.

Raising her in my arms, I signed to
Charlie to push the curtain aside which
hung at the back of the stage, and then I
carried her out of sight of the now shamed
and whispering audience.

At the back of the curtain were about a
dozen frightened men and woman in gaudy
tinselly dresses. They were all in a con-

dition of wild excitement, but none of them offered any help beyond directing us to the singer's dressing room, and thither Charlie and I pursued our way.

In the dressing room was a shabby sofa. On this I placed the poor moaning creature, and then Charlie gently drew the handkerchief from her face.

Merciful Heaven! Shall I ever forget that moment?

It was Hortense Guadella, my bitter implacable foe, who lay there, humbled and degraded, with a terrible gash in her forehead.

We recognised her at once, but I almost wonder that we did, for the alteration in her was awful. Wan and haggard, and worn almost to a skeleton, her fevered eyes glared with a wolfish gleam into mine; but presently, reading in my face the pity that filled my heart, the hard despairing eyes softened, and great tears rolled down the cheeks, mingling with the blood which still flowed from the ghastly wound upon the forehead.

With a faint cry the unfortunate woman
turned her face from me, and put up her
feeble hands to hide it.

"Friend Perditus," she moaned. "Oh,
Friend Perditus, if you have any mercy
leave me to die in peace. I injured you
cruelly, but heaven knows my punishment
is a heavy one."

We would not let her talk. With gentle
force Charlie insisted on bathing and bind-
ing up the injury to her forehead, while I
did what little I could to assist him and
to soothe her; but when it was all completed, to my inexpressible dismay, she
sank down at my feet, and bowing her
head, raised her hands in supplication
towards me.

"Forgive me, forgive me," she panted.
"Oh, Friend Perditus, you may do so, for
God has revenged your injury. I lied for
him, for my son, for Lucien. I wronged
you that he might be rich and happy. The
night we fled from you, on reaching Paris
he deserted me, carrying with him the

money and the jewels we had stolen from you."

"Oh, great heaven, what a villain!" I cried.

"Yes," she moaned, "he was a villain. I knew it; who so well? and yet I loved him."

"But you, how have you lived, then?"

"I can scarcely be said to have lived," she answered with a ghastly smile, "I have been starving more or less for the last two years; I have not eaten anything except a crust of bread for two days now. If I had been a success to-night I could have bought a supper; as it is—— "

She shrugged her shoulders, and for more than a minute there was silence in the room, so completely horrified was I.

Charlie and I took the suffering creature home to her poor lodgings, and then, after she had eaten and drank, I heard the rest of her wretched story.

It seemed that when her unspeakably atrocious son, Lucien, left her, there had been a struggle between them for the possession of the dressing-case containing the diamonds. During this struggle he had dealt her a dastardly blow, and from the effects of this blow she had been slowly but surely dying ever since.

Charlie and I broke out into exclamations of fury and pity when we heard of this appalling and unnatural act of wickedness, and then this most extraordinary woman raised her trembling hand and silenced us.

" You need not curse him," she said, " he has met with his deserts. Three months ago a body was found floating in the Seine with the blade of a dagger sheathed in its breast ; it was taken to the Morgue, and there I saw it. Friend Perditus, when I looked upon the dead body of the son for whom I had· sold my soul, my punishment was complete."

Hortense Guadella lived for two months, and I am thankful to know that some of her terrible sufferings were mitigated through my means.

As I write these parting words I am sitting by the open window of my library with my wife's head resting against my shoulder.

Looking upwards, I can see the vast blue dome of the sky with its countless myriads of twinkling stars. My heart swells within me with gratitude, and the peace of Heaven steals into my soul. Pressing my lips to my wife's, I murmur—

" Ah, my love, my dear love, thank God for His infinite mercies. I would that every one in this wide world were as happy as I am now ! "

THE END.

www.ingramcontent.com/pod-product-compliance
Lightning Source LLC
Chambersburg PA
CBHW020944030726
47496CB00005B/1349